Club Earth

Club Earth

GAIL GAUTHIER

G. P. Putnam's Sons • New York

Also by Gail Gauthier

My Life Among the Aliens

A Year with Butch and Spike

G. P. Putnam's Sons, a division of Penguin Putnam Books for Young Readers,
345 Hudson Street, New York, NY 10014.
G. P. Putnam's Sons, Reg. U.S. Pat. & Tm. Off.
Published simultaneously in Canada. Printed in the United States of America.
Book designed by Karen Robbins. Text set in Novarese.

Library of Congress Cataloging-in-Publication Data
Gauthier, Gail. ClubEarth / Gail Gauthier. p. cm.
Summary: When their house becomes a vacation resort for aliens
from other planets, Robby and Will enjoy the excitement before
finally finding a way to get rid of their free-loading guests.
[1. Extraterrestrial beings—Fiction. 2. Humorous stories.] I. Title.
II. Title: Club Earth. PZ7.G23435Cl 1999 [Fic]—dc21
98-31416 CIP AC ISBN 0-399-23373-3
1 3 5 7 9 10 8 6 4 2
First Impression

For Will and Rob—

Thanks for everything.

Contents

1
The Alien Who Came to Dinner

My father doesn't notice things.

In general, this is a very good trait in a parent. My father doesn't notice whether or not cereal has too much sugar or costs a lot of money. He just throws whatever we hand him into the shopping cart. Dad doesn't notice that my brother Robby and I are supposed to go to bed at exactly the time our favorite television show starts. If Mom's not around to ruin things, he'll even sit down and watch it with us. And he doesn't notice *anything* about our homework. In fact, I think he makes it a point not to.

I mention all this because it helps to explain how all the company we started having about a year and a half ago kind of got past him . . . and why he was so surprised when Sal came.

"Can we have someone stay for dinner?" I asked my mother late one snowy January afternoon after Robby and I came in from playing outside. Our mother *loves* to have company for dinner . . . or for breakfast, lunch, or anything at all. This is probably because, given a choice, few people are willing to eat at our place.

Not that day, though. "Dinner is going to have to be rushed because your father and I have a concert tonight," Mom said as she tried to look into the oven without opening the door all the way. "Did you forget?"

Forget that their guitar quartet was performing at a book store? Of *course*, we had.

"We'll eat fast," I pleaded. "And Saliva came such a long way."

Mom spun around and stared at the guy standing next to us dripping chunks of snow onto the kitchen floor. "Saliva?"

"I heard that word on the radio," Saliva explained. "Don't you just love the way it sounds?"

"I like 'spit' better, myself," Robby said.

Mom sort of collapsed against the kitchen counter. "Oh, no! Not tonight!" she wailed. "I wasn't expecting . . . Well, you did come a long way, I suppose. But all I have for dinner is zucchini bran pizza and marinated cucumber salad."

"Didn't we have something with cucumbers yesterday?" Robby complained. "And the day before?"

But ol' Sal just slapped the huge mittens he was wearing together and cried, "Cucumbers? I've been hearing about cucumbers for years! I never dreamed I'd actually get to *eat* one."

"Well, then," Mom sighed, "one of us is having a lucky day."

Sal looked out the window at the snow that had been falling for the last hour.

"I knew you people had only recently finished one of your ice ages," he said, "but I didn't realize how recently."

"Recently? The Ice Age has been over for billions of years," Robby corrected him as the three of us hauled our boots and coats out to the mud room.

Rob was only half way through third grade. He had a lot to learn.

"Try ten thousand years," I told him.

"Mom! Will's correcting me again," Robby whined through the door that led back to the kitchen.

"Ten thousand years or a billion, it's too close for comfort as far as I'm concerned . . . Oh, look!" Sal exclaimed as he pulled back the curtain on a window. "Something's sliding toward your house. At quite a good clip, too. Is it going to stop?"

"It" was my father sledding down our driveway in his twelve-year-old station wagon.

We wanted him to replace it with a truck—one of

those four-wheel drive sports utility vehicles that are supposed to take you anywhere in snowstorms or any other kind of weather. But Dad said, oh, no. Real men didn't need four-wheel drive.

"Just give me a good set of steel-belted radials," he said, "a snow shovel, a bucket of sand, twenty pounds of road salt, and a few dozen bricks in the back to provide traction, and I'll get us up Mt. Everest."

Which would be terrific if Mt. Everest were anywhere around here.

We backed out of the mud room just in time to make space for Dad.

"We're in for the ride of our lives tonight, Reggie," he called to my mother as he kicked off his boots.

"What I don't understand," Sal said, "is why you people keep talking about the weather but you never do anything about it. You'd think life forms that could put a man on a moon would be able to manage a little job like stopping a snowstorm."

Dad looked at Sal. Robby and I looked at Dad. Mom looked in the oven again.

"Dinner's ready," she announced.

"An alien's staying for dinner," Rob called over his shoulder to Dad as he raced into the dining room so he could take the chair next to Sal's.

"Really? R.J. Denis. Pleased to meet you," Dad said as he shook Sal's hand.

"I'm from one of the Anaspecifist planets. We don't

believe in labeling intelligent life forms. But if that makes you uncomfortable, you may call me either Saliva or Canned Tuna. I picked those words up on my scanner once as I was traveling through your air space. I just couldn't get them out of my mind," Sal explained.

"Anaspecifist planet, huh?" Dad repeated, a big grin on his face. "Are there a lot of those?"

"Not enough, if you want my opinion," Sal replied as he loaded his plate. And I mean *loaded*.

"I apologize for arriving unexpectedly. I understand that people on this world don't care much for surprises. However, I had to do a final inspection, and I couldn't very well warn you about that, now could I?"

Sal didn't wait for an answer. He leaned over his plate, took a deep breath, and sucked everything off from it with barely a sound.

"Ah, that was good," he sighed. Then he smiled.

"It's show time!" he announced. "Don't go anywhere. I'll be right back."

He jumped up and ran out the kitchen door.

"What a card! Where did you find him, Reggie? Is he a new guitar student? He seems a little old," Dad said to Mom.

"He's an alien, Dad," Rob told him. "Didn't you notice?"

"An alien," I repeated. "A-l-i-e-n."

"I know how to spell it." He turned to Mom. "So who is he?"

Mom just looked at Dad without saying anything.

"I'm impressed, Reg. I would never have believed you could carry off a joke like this. I mean . . ."

What he meant was that Mom doesn't have that great a sense of humor.

"You always think we're joking when we talk about the aliens who come here," Rob complained.

"That's because you are," Dad said with a big grin.

"No, Dad. *You* joke about aliens. We're always serious," I told him.

"You guys have to learn not to carry a joke on too long. The alien stuff was funny for a while . . . like for the first six or seven months you went on about it. But it's been over a year now that you two have been talking about space guys, and the joke is getting a little old now. I get it," Dad insisted.

"But you don't get it, Dad," I said.

Rob agreed. "You *so* don't get it."

Sal hurried back into the room with a skinny metal suitcase dripping with snow. With just a few motions he flipped the suitcase into a tripod with a good sized rectangular box at the top. Then he tapped the side of the box and it became a screen showing an aerial view of our house and yard.

"I bet you folks are wondering what brings me here. Well, I come bearing good news," he began, smiling at Mom and Dad. "Our research suggests that in spite of the fact that your planet is a little out-of-the-way and doesn't get a lot of intergalactic traffic, it is on the brink of being 'discovered' by the intergalactic recreation industry. That makes it a very desirable destination for those life forms that dislike crowds of mindless tourists. Crowds of mindless tourists can destroy a planet, as I'm sure you know."

"You bet!" Dad said just before he let out this big bark of a laugh. He quickly quieted down when no one joined him.

Sal pointed to the screen where we could see the trees between our house and the houses on each side of our yard. "You have the good fortune to own a lovely spot on this charming world. It's both isolated *and* a hub of activity for the locals."

He tapped the box again, and a picture of Robby and me playing Capture the Flag a while back with our friends and the two aliens Mom thought were new kids named Leo and Fred flashed by.

"You laughed when we told you Leo and Fred were space men," I reminded Dad. "You never noticed we weren't joking."

"It's a center for culture," Saliva continued as a picture of my father playing his electric guitar at my ninth birthday party came up on the screen.

Dad stared at the scene. He looked the way he does when he's sitting at the top of the Sudden Death slide at the water park.

"Yet the friendly natives are also ready to provide

any service required," Sal went on. And there I was throwing Dad's antique pulley up over a tree limb in an attempt to lift a rock off from an alien's spaceship.

"So that's how that thing broke?" Dad whispered. His face looked just the way it does after he's just been down the chute and is staggering toward the steps so he can go down the slide again.

"I wasn't joking when I told you about that, either," I grumbled. I had been in trouble for days over that broken pulley, and all I had been trying to do was be helpful.

"The food rates four stars." Picture after picture came up of bran muffins, mushroom-broccoli soup, carob-whole-wheat brownies, pumpkin-oatmeal cookies, frozen orange juice and yogurt pops, cracked wheat bread smeared with homemade, natural peanut butter, and vegetable stuffed pitas, fajitas, tacos, manicottis, popovers—in short, all the things our alien visitors had loved, but humans eat only to prevent starvation. There was even a picture of the zucchini bran pizza Mom had taken out of the oven just a few minutes earlier.

Sal tapped the tripod one more time and a front view of our house—looking unusually nice, by the way—turned up on the screen. "In short, you people have the makings here of a first-class resort," he explained as the words Club Earth appeared floating over our roof. "My clients are going to love it here."

"Your clients?" I repeated.

"The ones who are going to pay me so they can come stay with you," Sal explained.

"We're going to run a hotel!" I shrieked.

Sal corrected me. "We prefer the word 'lodge.' It suggests something rustic and rural, which this place certainly is."

"No, no, no," Mom said from where she was still sitting behind her untouched dinner plate. "I don't mind a visitor—or two or three—every now and then, but I am *not* going to run a resort."

"Mom! We'd be the only people we know having aliens sleep over!" Robby wailed.

"You'd be the only people on Earth having aliens sleep over," Sal assured him.

Dad looked at me and grinned foolishly. "That would be pretty cool, wouldn't it?"

"This isn't a joke, R.J.! Can't you tell he's serious? He's talking about *aliens*! Beings from other planets! Here in our house! H*e* is an alien. Here in our house. Is 'That would be pretty cool' all you can say?" Mom demanded.

"Just about," Dad said. "Words fail me, Regina. I'm . . . I'm just stunned by . . . ah . . . just the idea of life on . . . on other worlds. Yeah. That's it. I'm stunned . . . by . . . HOW COOL THIS IS!"

Then Dad started laughing and pounding the table. Robby jumped up and hugged him. "I knew you'd love them, Dad."

"No, no, no," Mom said again. "We don't have time to

have guests running in and out of here. I don't care who loves them."

Dad suddenly sobered up. "I hope what I'm about to ask you isn't rude or anything," he said to Sal, "but these clients of yours—they won't be higher on the food chain than we are, will they?"

Robby shrieked and I said, "We're the top of the food chain on this planet. We eat everything, but nothing eats us. You're not going to send anyone here who's going to think 'coming for lunch' means . . . ?"

"Not to worry. You might get a few parasites staying over now and then, but they would never be so rude as to eat their hosts," Sal assured us.

"And will they have two legs, two arms, two of everything you're supposed to have two of *where* you're supposed to have them?" Rob asked. "We're not going to have spider people here, are we?"

"I'm not aware of any spider people who like to travel," Sal replied. "And if they did, they wouldn't come here. The only tourists who are going to want to come to Earth are going to be members of species whose ancestors evolved in similar ways to yours. Spider people, residents of gas planets . . . they're not coming to Earth. Not on vacation, anyway," Sal promised.

Dad turned to Mom. "Isn't this great?" he exclaimed happily.

"No, it is not. Houseguests mean a lot of extra cooking and cleaning. Has anyone thought about who is going to do all that extra work?"

"You are, Mom," Robby replied. "Duh!"

"What's cleaning a few bathrooms and doing a few extra loads of laundry compared to what the aliens will be doing—traveling bazillions of miles through space and time warps and black holes and whatever?" Dad asked.

"You wouldn't ask that question if you'd ever actually cleaned a bathroom or done a load of laundry," Mom said.

"We'll take care of them," I offered quickly. "We'll do all the extra work. I swear we will."

Mom gave me a look that said she was not impressed. "Will, that's what you and Robby said about the fish you wanted a couple of years ago. You remember how that turned out?"

The thought of flushing a dead alien down the toilet did not make for a pretty picture.

"Reggie, we have an opportunity here to meet forms of life no one else has ever known. This is our chance to do something big, bigger than anything we've ever imagined," Dad said.

"And it would be educational, Mom," I suggested. "Maybe Rob and I could learn a foreign language."

I knew I had her there. Mothers love educational stuff, especially if it's for kids and not them.

"Please! Please! Please, Mommy!" Robby cried. He tried to look cute but didn't do too good a job. "We'll be famous!"

"That's not a good argument, not a good argument at

all," Sal said. "You won't be famous because you can't tell anyone about this."

"And how are we supposed to keep the presence of alien life a secret?" Mom asked.

"We had aliens coming here for a year before you knew about them," I reminded her. "And we *tried* to tell you."

"But they were only coming once in a while and staying long enough to get something to eat," Mom objected. "You're talking about having creatures . . . I'm sorry, um, beings . . . move in and stay for days at a time, aren't you? How are we supposed to keep that a secret? What will we tell people?"

"We're not talking some rinky-dink set up like Disney World that lets in just anybody," Sal explained. "You're not going to have an alien presence here all the time. Club Earth will be reserved for only the finest customers. There aren't going to be that many who can afford to make the trip or stay for very long. Tell people that your guests are relatives."

"Why all the secrecy?" Dad asked. "Why don't you want anyone to know you're here?"

I knew. "Some secret Earth agency will come and take away the aliens. Our doctors will perform tests on them and keep them locked up so scientists from all over the world can come and stare at them."

Sal looked at Dad and laughed. "That one's got an imagination, hasn't he? No, young man, beings who have conquered interstellar travel have nothing to fear from your Dark Age M.D.s. You need to keep our presence a secret to protect your planet."

"I don't get it," said Robby. "Protect our planet from what?"

"From my competitors," Sal said nastily. "Do you know what some folks in the extraterrestrial travel field would do to a newly discovered vacation area like Earth? Overrun it. You'll wake up one morning and find an intergalactic fast food outlet operating on every corner. Acres and acres of land will be paved for star cruiser parks. You'll have life forms living out of their space vehicles for a couple of months at a time, after which the land they're parked on won't be good for anything for the better part of a century. And you should see what some of these organisms play for miniature golf." He shuddered.

"Oh, well," Rob said. "So we won't be famous. At least we'll be rich."

"You won't be that, either," Sal objected.

"Why not? All these space guys will be paying us so they can come here."

Sal corrected Rob. "They'll be paying *me* so they can come here."

"And we'll be working for you, so you'll be paying us," I said.

"Why would I do that?" Sal asked, sounding shocked.

"Because it's the fair thing to do," I told him.

" 'Fair.' I'm not familiar with that word. Can you explain it to me?"

"Fair—it means right or honest," I began. "Or—"

"It means," Robby broke in, "that if someone works for you, you pay them."

Sal shook his head. "That must be some kind of Earth thing. I've never heard of it."

Mom and Dad gave each other a look.

"We can afford a few extra meals for a hungry space traveler," Mom said. "But the secrecy—it's too great a responsibility. We're going to have to say no."

"But you can't say no," Sal pointed out.

Something in his tone of voice made all of us become very still and start watching him carefully.

"What do you mean?" Dad asked.

"You just can't."

Suddenly things were beginning to look kind of grim.

"Of course we can," Mom declared.

"Careful, Mom," Robby warned. "Don't you know about the awful things aliens can do to humans? They can kidnap them and study their bodies and stick little metal things up their noses and . . . "

Sal rolled his eyes in disgust. "Humans are so conceited. They think everyone wants to know all about them. I can tell you on very good authority, no one cares. There isn't a life form in this galazy that wants to stick little metal things up your noses." He paused. "Well, maybe one."

Mom stood up. Dad signaled to us to move to the back of the dining room. Then he got out of his chair and stood next to Mom.

"We don't want to do this," Mom said after we had all taken our positions.

"I think I have something here that will change your mind," Sal said as he hit the box on the top of the tripod again.

The front page of our Grandma Judy's favorite newspaper, *The Investigator*, appeared. Big letters across the top of the page said, "Cure For Cancer Could Be In Your Cat's Litter Box!" A smaller headline claimed, "Scientists Agree: Forty-Pound Five-Month-Old Is Bigfoot's Baby!" And right across from that was another title that said, "Family Claims Aliens Sleep At Their House!"

The pages of *The Investigator* flipped to page five where another headline stated, "Family Of Four Approached By Aliens." Under it was a picture of my mother, father, Robby, and me. We had these big, creepy smiles on our faces. We looked as if a dentist had just asked us to show him our teeth. Our eyes were popping, and we were wearing those headbands with the really fake looking antennae sticking off the top of them.

"Whoa, Reggie!" Dad exclaimed. "That is *not* a good picture of you."

Dad didn't seem to notice that he didn't exactly look like a prince, either.

A voice from the box began to read the story.

"R.J. Denis, *owner of* Denis' Music, *and his wife*, Regina, *a guitar instructor, musician, and housewife, claim they were contacted by extraterrestrials who wanted to use their home as a bed and breakfast stop for vacationing spacemen and women*!

" '*They had been visiting with my sons off and on for over a year,*' *Regina explains.* '*They liked our home—and my cooking, I might add—so much that they decided they'd like to vacation here.*'

"*Younger son Robert claims the space dudes were all harmless and no threat to anyone.* '*It would have been great to have aliens sleeping at our house. My mother was just too lazy to cook and clean for them.*' "

We all looked at Robby.

"I didn't say that!" he complained.

I bet he would have, though.

The voice from the box continued: "*Older son William explains that the aliens required absolute secrecy about their presence.* '*They were worried that too many aliens would want to come here for vacations if word got around that this was a nice spot for aliens to visit. I don't know what's going to happen now that the secret is out.*'

"*Regina Denis admits that by blowing the whistle on the alien plan she may have risked having the Earth overrun by extraterrestrials looking for a good time.* '*It was the only way I could think of to get the aliens out of my house.*'

"*Officials at the Pentagon were contacted about the possible threat of an invasion of alien tourists. A spokesperson said,* '*This isn't a scenario we have ever considered. The Earth is totally unprepared.*' "

"Oh, come on," Dad laughed. "Nobody's going to believe that. They'll think we're like those people who wear spaghetti strainers on their heads to keep evil scientists from X-raying their brains. It'll be a big joke."

Mom slowly sat back down on her chair. "I won't be laughing."

"Hmmm. What is it you people call what I'm doing to you?" Sal asked. "I can never remember the right word."

"Blackmail," Mom sighed. "And I'd rather you stuck metal things up my nose."

"Do I take it we have a deal?" Sal asked.

Mom nodded her head.

"You won't be sorry," Sal promised as he folded up his tripod. "I'll take care of reservations. Your guests will show up much as they have in the past. Believe me, you won't even notice they're here."

2
It's a Bird! It's a Plane! It's an Alien!

Once my father decided to believe in aliens it was as if he had never not believed in them. The same kind of thing must have happened when people decided to believe the world is round. They were probably embarrassed that they ever thought it was flat and tried not to mention it much. Dad always tried to change the subject whenever we brought up how he used to laugh when we talked about the aliens visiting us.

But when weeks passed with no aliens dropping by, we all began to worry about other things. Snow days, for instance. Week after week of winter was passing without school closing because of snow. Not that we weren't getting plenty of the stuff—between three in the afternoon and nine at night. It always seemed to start just as we were getting off the bus in front of our house and stop as we were getting into bed. The end of February came and went, and we had been to school *every single day*. Even the teachers were getting worried that they wouldn't get any extra time off.

Finally, at the end of March, long after everyone had given up hoping, we got up to find we could have stayed in bed. Snow was coming down so heavily and so steadily it was hard to see how you could breath outdoors without inhaling it.

"This is just like the planet in the *Global Battalion*!" Robby shouted as we headed for No Mom's Land, the area between our yard and our neighbors', the O.'s. No Mom was sure who owned it, so No Mom cleaned it up. No Mom even cared what happened out there so long as there were no injuries involving stitches.

"What are you doing?" Tommy O. shouted from his bedroom window.

"We belong to the Global Battalion and we're building a barricade to protect our home world from ice monsters!" I called back through the wall of snow that was pouring out of the sky.

"I'll be right there."

In just minutes Tom was tearing out of his garage with a big trash can, a shovel, and his younger brother,

Danny. They were filling the trash can with snow so they could make turrets for our barricade when their sister Katie appeared with a spatula. She started carving little spaces into the top of the wall so we could spray colored water through them at our attackers.

"Okay," I began, "I'm Lieutenant Laser, and I—"

"I want to be Lieutenant Laser," Robby objected.

"I said it first," I pointed out.

"The *Global Battalion* comic books belong to me, so I should be their leader, Lieutenant Laser," Robby reasoned.

"That's a stupid reason. I'll be Lieutenant Laser," Katie offered. "Then you won't have to fight about it."

"You can't be Lieutenant Laser. You're a girl!" Robby told her. "You'll have to be Laser's sister."

"The one who's going out with that weird guy from the *Solar Commandos* comics? No way!" Katie said.

"Will or I should be Lieutenant Laser," Tom announced. "We're the oldest. Actually, we shouldn't even be playing a make-believe game at all. But if we're going to, we should at least be the boss."

Robby said he wasn't going to play if he couldn't be Lieutenant Laser.

"I'll be Lieutenant Laser, Tom will be Comrade Cutlass, and you can be the guy Laser's sister is dating," I told him. "Laser doesn't like him, so that way I can beat you up."

Robby snorted. "Except that you *can't* beat me up."

"What about me?" Danny O. asked. "Who will I be?"

"You can be all the other guys in the battalion," I promised him. "Unless some other kids show up to play. Then we'll have to give them some of the parts, and you can be the Pickax."

Danny had just learned to read and really didn't know that much about the *Battalion*. So it wasn't very hard to convince him that Pickax, who used to be evil but had learned the error of his ways after being saved by Lieutenant Laser from the deadly coils of the Electric Eel, was a good part to play.

"Stop!" I ordered when we were finally ready to begin. "Listen. What's that sound?"

"It's Grandpa cleaning our driveway with his snow blower," Danny replied.

"No, it's not. It's the rumble of the ice monsters. They're on the move," Robby explained. "There are thousands of them."

"They eat human flesh, you know," Tom said.

"Not, if we eat them first!" Robby yelled.

Katie waved her spatula in the air. "They'll never take us alive!" she shouted.

That was when we started screaming. "Melt 'em!" "Where's my flame-thrower!" "I'm freezing!" "They're everywhere!" "I'll shoot any coward who runs!" Danny kept reminding everyone about what we were supposed to be doing by just shouting, "Ice monsters! Ice monsters!"

"Ice monsters?" somebody wailed, sounding really scared. "Here? No! Say it isn't so!"

Suddenly, someone was trying to crawl in between two large rocks.

"You're going to get stuck," I warned.

"We have to do something," a muffled voice replied. "The most horrible creatures in the cosmos are coming here to destroy us."

"Don't worry. We'll make cubes out of them!" Robby promised.

The newcomer, who realized he hadn't chosen a very good hiding place, gave up and struggled back onto his knees. A huge, fur-rimmed hood came down over his head, and his parka was so large that he looked as if all he had to do was squat down to create a tent whenever he wanted one.

"There is a way to beat ice monsters," he said suddenly. "I read about it in a book. You have to get down low so they can't see you. Then you have to trip them. When they hit the ground, they break."

Robby looked at him suspiciously. "I never saw that in *Global Battalion*."

"But it's good," Tom insisted. "It's real good."

"Let's all get down on our hands and knees," Katie suggested.

"Now what do we do?" Danny asked after we were all down in the snow.

"We wait for the ice monsters," the guy in the hood said.

"How long will that take?" Tom asked.

"I don't know. How far away are they?" the guy said.

"It was Will and Robby's idea," Danny answered.

"Well," I began hesitantly, "I don't know how far away they are. How far away do we want them to be?"

We all pretty much agreed we really didn't care how far away the ice monsters were—except for the new guy who said that, given a choice, he'd prefer they'd be on the other side of the galaxy.

And the rest of us said yeah, that was okay with us.

"So the ice monsters aren't coming? Then I'm going in," Danny announced.

Katie followed him inside, and Tom's grandfather shouted for him to come home so he could help shovel snow.

That left three of us in No Mom's Land, which was one more than we'd started with that morning.

"So that's all there is to ending an attack on this planet? You just decide the enemy is somewhere else?" the extra somebody asked.

Robby and I looked at each other and nodded.

"Pretty much," I said.

"Hmmm. It didn't make us late for lunch, did it?"

"Mom!" Robby shouted when we got in the house.

"I'm downstairs in the playroom."

"Come here."

"I'm practicing. You're not supposed to interrupt me when I'm practicing."

"You better come here, Mom," Robby called anyway.

"Later."

"He's right, Mom. You better come," I shouted.

The last chord we heard didn't sound too good. Then Mom stomped up the stairs and said, "What do you guys think I am, anyway, your personal slave?"

"You keep slaves on this planet? I didn't think anybody did that in this part of the galaxy anymore."

Mom gasped and covered her mouth with her hands. "You can't come today! It's a snow day!" she finally croaked at the space guy. "I haven't done anything!"

"What were you supposed to do?"

"Empty the dish washer, do two loads of laundry, clean the oven, vacuum the hall and the stairs . . . " Mom paused to look down at her nightgown. "Get dressed."

The alien looked at me and nodded. "So you *do* keep slaves here. What a great idea."

I thought so, too.

"What's your name?" I asked our guest as he lumbered ahead of us down to the laundry room to put our snow pants in the dryer while Mom got dressed.

"I've heard about your race's need to label things, and I am prepared," he said as he pulled off his enormous parka. "You may call me Lard Butt."

"Did you say Lard . . . B . . . B . . . Bu . . . Butt?" I stammered.

"That's right. Somebody want to give me a hand getting out of these things?"

"These things" were a pair of purple snow pants that were stretched across, well, they were stretched across what Robby later said was the biggest butt he'd ever seen in his life. And since he spent a lot of time staring at it while we were in the laundry room, he ought to know.

"On this planet," Robby gasped as we struggled to peel Lard Butt's snow pants off him, "the words Lard Butt have sort of a strange meaning."

"Oh, no," Lard Butt grunted. "I chose them because I thought they meant big backside, and I have this big . . . "

He suddenly popped like a cork out of his snow pants. Robby and I ended up in a heap on the floor with the pants.

"That's the strange meaning I was thinking of," Robby said.

"Good," Lard Butt said. He had on a pair of those light gray sweatpants, the nice ones with a drawstring around the waist instead of just elastic. They looked brand new and as if he'd had them specially made because I had never seen a pair before that didn't have grape juice or ketchup stains on them or were that big.

"It's a great name," Robby told him. "It's exactly what I would have chosen for you."

Lard Butt looked pleased. "Thanks."

"I'm telling Mom what he calls himself," I whispered as Lard Butt waddled ahead of us up the stairs.

"Forget it. You were Lieutenant Laser, so I get to tell."

"I said it first," I said, sounding really nasty, I thought. "You're always . . . "

We were at the top of the stairs by then, and we could

see my mother smiling at Lard Butt with this really stiff, surprised look on her face as she said, "Why, what a lovely name! And I'm Regina Denis." That pretty much put an end to my fight with Robby, but I sort of nudged him into the wall anyway just to let him know I could have won.

Unfortunately, Mom was trying to look anywhere but at Lard Butt's backside and caught me in the act. She caught Robby elbowing me back, too. So she made me pull out all twenty-five feet of the central vacuum hose just so I could vacuum the hall for her, and Robby had to empty the dishwasher. (Robby always gets the easy jobs.) Lard Butt said we had a thing or two to learn about how to treat slaves. As we were sitting down to lunch he gave us this long description of how the miners on Yttrium 7 treat theirs. It was very interesting, but I didn't think it was very likely Mom would let us put an electrically charged ring in her ear.

"Here's a napkin for you," Mom said to Lard Butt as she handed him a dish towel to spread over his lap. It should have been a bath towel, of course. Heck, it should have been a bed sheet. Lard Butt covered one and a half of our dining room chairs once he was seated.

He sniffed his lunch. It was one of Mom's thin green soups and fat slices of brown bread with chunks of sprouted seeds sticking out of them like little tentacles.

"I have a delicate stomach, you know. You were warned about that, weren't you?" he asked Mom.

I have a delicate stomach. It can't tolerate weird

grains or any kind of bean that's not a string bean or too many raw vegetables. (A fancy word for raw vegetables is crudités, the first four letters of which spell *crud*. That says it all.) But does my mother ever make me the canned pasta and frozen pizza a growing boy needs? She does not. And I'm her own flesh and blood. So you'd think a member of another species would have no hope at all of finding something edible at our house.

That's what you'd think anyway.

"Fine chef you have here," Lard Butt said as he patted the last drop of soup from around his mouth. "I don't suppose you'd consider selling her?"

"How much you willing to pay?" Robby asked.

They got into a big discussion about how much the money on Lard Butt's planet was worth in Earth dollars that only ended when I reminded Robby that one of the Ten Commandments says you can't sell your parents.

After lunch Lard Butt headed for the couch in the living room. We could hear the springs under the cushions popping from down the hall where we were squeezing into the bathroom with Mom who was rushing to decontaminate the bathtub.

"Who got in this tub with his boots on?" she asked. "How do you two get this thing so dirty? Would someone hand me that sponge over there?"

"Will can do it," Rob said.

"It's wet! It may have been in the toilet. I don't want to touch it!" I yelled at him.

"You know, I've heard that the Hurst kids have to clean the bathrooms at their house," Mom grunted as she stretched to grab the sponge herself. "They touch wet sponges all the time."

"That's because Mrs. Hurst works. Those kids have to do all kinds of stuff," I explained. Picturing some of the stuff Kevin Hurst had to do brought an awful thought to my mind.

"You're not thinking about going to work, are you?" I asked.

"I already work," Mom claimed as she scrubbed away at the bottom of the tub.

"Not really," Robby said. "You don't do anything important."

If I had been Rob, I would have ducked because it looked as if Mom was going to throw that sponge right at his head. Instead, she just asked why we were bothering her when we had a guest to entertain.

"We want to know if we have to spend our whole afternoon with him," I explained.

Mom collapsed against the side of the tub, then turned and looked at us. "You don't want to? I thought having aliens come to stay was *exactly* what you wanted? How did you put it? 'Please! Please! Please, Mommy?' "

"He said that," I reminded her, pointing at Robby. "I didn't."

"I didn't mean they should come on our snow day," Rob explained. "This may be the only one we get."

"But you didn't say you wanted aliens to come here just when it was convenient for you," Mom pointed out.

"That's what we meant," Robby said. "I thought everyone realized that."

Mom laughed. "You thought wrong. But how about if I make a deal with you? I'll spend the afternoon entertaining Mr. Butt if you finish cleaning the two bathrooms, do the laundry, clean the oven, and make dinner."

In just seconds we were back in the living room. We found Lard Butt stretched out on the couch with a copy of *Global Battalion* held up in front of his face.

"This is incredible," he said as he turned a page. "I've just read three of these books. The writers on this world . . . what a way they have with words! Listen to this! 'FOOM!' 'POW!' 'WHAM!' I know good writing when I see it, and that is GOOD writing."

"You think that's good? That's nothing!" Robby exclaimed as he ran back down the hall to his bedroom. When he came back, he had as many back copies of *Global Battalion* and *Solar Commandos* as he could carry.

"Issue twenty-nine of the *Global Battalion* is my all time favorite," he explained as he dug through the clear plastic bags that held individual issues of our comic books. "Here it is. It's about how Toaster and Astro Bowler joined the *Battalion* after Toaster's spaceship crash-landed on Earth."

"I noticed in your other books that there are a lot of

nonhuman beings here on Earth who have abnormal powers. I've never heard of that on any other planet. It must be something about Earth's atmosphere," Lard Butt said as he took issue twenty-nine from Rob.

"Actually . . ." I began.

"What I can't get over are the pictures. Pictures to go along with a story! It's unheard of! Whoever travels around with these super heroes and mutants so they can draw them has one great job!" Lard Butt said, nodding his head.

"Artists don't travel with them," I tried to explain.

"You mean these are photographs?" Lard Butt asked. "Very impressive."

"No. One person writes the story and someone else draws pictures to go along with it. You see?" I said.

Lard Butt nodded his head. "So only the authors really travel with the Global Battalion and the Solar Commandos, and they write up what they see and tell the artists what to draw."

"Yes," Robby agreed.

"No! Robby, there is no Global Battalion and there are no Solar Commandos! You know that," I reminded.

"Oh, that's right. I got confused for a minute. Everything is made up," he told Lard Butt.

Lard Butt laughed. "Trying to pull a little joke on a poor vacationing alien, are you? You'll have to try that one on someone else. When I said I knew good writing, I meant I *knew* good writing. I'm an author, myself, and I know that authors don't make anything up. They write from their own experience." He tapped issue twenty-nine with one finger. "The writer of this story knew what he was talking about."

We looked down at the page Lard Butt had been reading. It was all about how Red Kelly became Astro Bowler after the Toaster's space ship landed on the bowling alley where Red worked when he wasn't winning bowling tournaments.

"Ya think?" Robby asked me.

"No, I don't think! Use your head, Rob! Nobody captures bad guys by knocking them on the noggin with rocket-powered bowling balls and shouting 'Strike!' "

"It would be cool, though, wouldn't it?" he said sadly.

"If it happened. Which it doesn't," I told him.

Lard Butt sat up and something under one end of the couch gave way altogether, causing him to sink a couple of inches.

"Let me explain to you boys how writing works. I'll use my most famous piece of work, *The Bottomless Pits On Boron*, as an example. I traveled to Boron, where I was directed to their famous bottomless pits. I walked along the edge—you know, right along the top so I could look over the side into them—until I got tired. Then I turned around and walked along until I got back where I started."

"And?" Robby asked when Lard Butt appeared to be finished. "Was there anything in the pits?"

"How would I know? They're bottomless. I won a Wurlitzer Award for that story. And when I write up what happened this morning when the ice monsters didn't attack, I'll win another."

"There were no ice monsters here this morning," I reminded him.

"You don't have to tell me. I was there. 'Chilling'—that's what the critics on my world are going to call the story of how Earth just missed being overrun by ice monsters. I'm going to see if I can find someone to draw pictures to go along with it. What color would you say your hair is?" he asked me.

Robby smiled. "We can prove to you that comic books are made up," he said as he got up and left the room again.

"Look," he said when he came back. He was holding a wire-bound tablet of drawing paper. "Will and I are writing a comic book. And we're making it all up. Every word."

What he had in his hand was volume one, issue one, of the *Planetary Patrol*, about a platoon of warriors who travel from planet to planet protecting the innocent from the forces of Colonel John Grimm, an American astronaut whose space capsule had been bombarded with radiation making him both immortal and evil at the same time. We had been working on it for weeks.

"The pictures in your comic compared to the ones in the others . . . they really stink," Lard Butt said.

"Robby made them," I explained.

"I haven't been to college yet to learn how to draw,

you know," Rob complained. "And I haven't put the coloring in yet. They'll look a lot better with color."

"This book's a lot shorter than the others, too," Lard Butt pointed out.

"That's Will's fault," Rob said. "He's supposed to be doing the story, but he can't think of one."

"It's hard to think of a super hero who hasn't already been thought of," I answered. "And whenever I do get an idea, you don't like it."

"A super hero who uses his rotten breath to gas bad guys, Will? That's not an idea, it's a joke," Robby complained.

"It was a great idea. A lot of super heroes are very sad people because their super powers make it hard for them to make friends. If I had breath so bad it made people pass out, I'd be pretty unhappy," I insisted.

"You *do* have breath that bad, and it never bothers you at all," Robby said.

"You're having these problems because you're trying to make up the story instead of writing one that's actually happened," Lard Butt broke in. "You have to find a super hero and spend some time with him."

"Lard Butt, you've got to listen to me. There *are no super heroes*," I said, being careful to stress every word.

Lard Butt waved a hand at the comics spread around on the couch and floor. "These authors didn't have any trouble finding some."

We were interrupted by the telephone. Dad was calling from a house up at the end of our street where he had, in spite of his steel-belted radials, snow shovel, bucket of sand, twenty pounds of road salt, and dozens of bricks, got the station wagon stuck in a snow bank.

"We were born too late, that's the problem," I complained as the three of us left our driveway and started up the street to meet Dad. "All the good super heroes and mutants have been taken."

"Yeah," Robby agreed. "Some of these comic book characters are getting awfully complicated. They control peoples' minds with weird chemicals they make in their bodies and are involved in wars I can't understand with groups of people I've never heard of. We need a simple hero like Superman. He just bounces bullets off his chest, looks through walls with his X-ray vision and flies. That's all easy stuff."

"Why don't you talk to this Superman?" Lard Butt suggested. "Maybe he knows someone you could write about. I've noticed that a lot of these comic book heroes know one another."

We would have told Lard Butt why we couldn't talk to Superman but by then we couldn't miss the sound of our station wagon's engine revving as Dad held the gas pedal to the floor hoping a miracle would occur and he'd back out of the ditch he'd driven into. A few minutes later, we picked up the unmistakable smell of burning rubber.

"That's your father in there pounding that wheel like that?" Lard Butt asked as he peered through the window in the car door. "It looks as if he's saying something."

"Yeah," I said. "But you probably don't want to know what it is."

Dad rolled down his window.

"Look, Dad! An alien!" Rob said, pointing at Lard Butt.

"Keep him away from this car. I'm going to come tearing out of here any minute, and I don't want anyone to get hurt!" Dad yelled.

I looked over at the front of the station wagon, which was pretty much buried in snow. I wasn't worried about getting hurt.

It was fun, for a while, standing there with the snow coming down all around us and thc bluc hazc from thc station wagon's exhaust billowing up like a cloud.

"And how long does this particular form of entertainment last?" Lard Butt finally asked.

"Usually? A long time. A long, long time," Robby answered.

I looked up at the sky. "It's going to get dark soon," I said.

Lard Butt didn't reply. He just hauled himself up over the snow bank and stood in front of the car. He stood there for a moment, and then began to twirl his hips and butt in a clockwise circle that got bigger and bigger, picking up speed and power along the way. Dad was looking over his shoulder to make certain that when he came "tearing out" of there he wouldn't hit any other cars in the street. So it's safe to say that when Lard Butt launched his backside against the front of the wagon like a boulder careening out of a slingshot, my father never knew what hit him. Nor would he ever know how he ended up back out in the street.

"That was fantastic!" Robby exclaimed.

"Ah, it was nothing," Lard Butt said modestly over his shoulder as he headed back toward our house. "There are thirty million butts like this on my home world. Any one of them could have done what I did."

I grabbed Robby's arm and made him stop to listen to me. "There are thirty million butts like that on his world, but only one on *ours*."

Robby's eyes popped. "Super Butt," he whispered.

I shook my head. "The Butt Lord—With His Butt Of Steel."

"Yes!" Robby said, grinning. "I like it!"

And so did I.

3
How Aliens Have Fun

Usually, when you think of aliens coming to Earth you think about them pulverizing the Pentagon or bombing Buckingham Palace. You don't think of them wrecking one of your mother's couches. Dad couldn't understand how it happened. He said Lard Butt's backside being the size it was, the pounds of pressure per square foot shouldn't have been all that great. Fortunately, Lard Butt dozed off on the couch for a while after dinner, thought it was morning when he woke up, and left. If he'd spent the night on the little fold-out sofa in the sunroom, we'd have had to cut it up for kindling.

After that first guest arrived, Mom went nuts mopping floors and cleaning drawers. The next alien wasn't going to catch her unprepared, she told us. Aliens had been coming to see Rob and me for a long time without our lifting a finger so we figured that we would just do what we'd always done to get ready for them, which was nothing. That wasn't good enough for our mother, though. She said we were our planet's ambassadors and had to make a good impression, which could only happen if our dirty underwear was not left lying on the floor. She also said Rob had to wash the tops of all the spice jars in the spice rack. I had to put away all of the videotapes piled on the floor next to the TV. She got Dad to clean the tile in both shower stalls and put new grout around the bathtub.

We told them we'd never heard of an alien taking a shower or a bath, but Dad said he supposed anyone who spent more than a day on our world would want to.

Mom had everyone in the family scrubbing and dusting through our spring break, our last school field trips, and our class picnics. And it was all a lot of wasted effort because, except for our cousin Brendan and Aunt Connie who came for dinner at Easter, no one unusual showed up.

"What if aliens are offended by cleanliness?" I argued one day the week after school let out while Rob and I were in the cellar with our father. Dad had left his assistant manager to run the music store for the afternoon so he could stay with us while Mom gave a kids' concert at a library. "What if they think Lestoil is some kind of chemical weapon and will launch an attack on our world if they smell it when they come into our house? We could be doing all this work just to cause some kind of intergalactic incident."

"Good point," Dad said. "We'll just forget about using Lestoil while we clean this closet."

"Why don't we just forget about cleaning the closet, too?" Robby suggested.

"Because it's my closet, and I love to clean it," Dad said. He drew out the word love so it lasted a long time and rubbed his hands together.

"When Mom said to clean the closet, she didn't mean this one, Dad. She meant the one in the upstairs hall. The one where you put all the clothes that don't fit you anymore and the socks you've lost the mates to. The one with all the cans of pennies you've been saving. The one with all the old magazines you're going to read some day when you've got time. The one with all the batteries that might work but probably don't. The one that smells like an old—"

Rob interrupted me. "That couldn't have been what she meant. We must have heard her wrong."

"That's right," Dad agreed. "Your mother probably wants to clean that one herself . . . sometime when I'm at work. Besides, when I told her I'd clean a closet, I meant *my* closet."

Dad's closet isn't a closet at all but a space under our cellar stairs that my parents had built a wall in front of. It's where he keeps his professional, high quality things—a half dozen old speakers in a variety of sizes and colors, three record turntables no one in the world wants, and a reel to reel tape recorder, like the ones you see in some of the original *Twilight Zones*, for instance. He also has every Walkman anyone in our family has ever owned, whether it works or not. There are two stereo receivers in the closet, a hand full of those little headphones, and a cassette player that my grandfather pulled out of an old car. Dad has his first electric guitar down there (which is probably valuable seeing as it's so old), one of those mirrored balls they used to hang over dance floors, and a few miles of antenna wire.

It was real cool stuff, and every now and then we liked to pull it all out and look at it for a while. That's what we were doing when a voice from somewhere above us called, "Is this the Recreation Hall?"

I went to the bottom of the stairs and looked up. A figure about as tall as the duffel bag propped on the floor beside it stood in the doorway.

"I have my registration form," he said. Then he made his way toward me, dragging his possessions behind him.

"Dad," I said.

"If that's Tom, tell him he can come on down. We'll

put him to work when it's time to put these things away."

There was a thumping noise as the duffel bag hit each step.

"It's not Tom."

Dad came to the bottom of the stairs, too. "Whoa! What's this?"

Robby peered under Dad's elbow. "It's an alien," he said.

The alien handed Dad something that looked like a piece of paper except that it was soft and limp like a handkerchief. There were words typed on it as neatly as if it—the paper or handkerchief—had gone through a printer.

NAME (if you have one): JD100
HOME PLANET: $NaHCO_3$
PARENTS: Cl17 and F9
SPECIAL HEALTH PROBLEMS: If rash develops, apply sodium carbonate
FAVORITE ACTIVITIES: Plays well by himself
IN CASE OF EMERGENCY NOTIFY: He's going to Earth. There are no emergencies there.

"I think there's been a mistake," Dad said. "This looks like a camp form."

JD100 agreed that it did.

"This isn't a camp," Robby said, his voice rising the

way it does just before he melts down. "It's an intergalactic resort. Or a lodge. But it's definitely not a camp."

"The life form that accepted my registration called this place Club Earth. My father said it sounded like a camp he went to in the Actinoid cluster. He said he had a very good time there."

As he spoke, JD100 wandered around a little, looking into the laundry room, around the playroom, and into the little door leading into Dad's still empty closet.

"Is this my cabin?" he asked.

"Your *cabin*!" Robby howled. "I'm the one who should be sleeping in a *cabin*. I've wanted to go to camp for years . . ."

"Not now, Rob," Dad warned.

"That's what you say every year! I'm told I have to wait until I'm twelve, but someone who just stepped onto the planet gets to go right away? How do you explain that?"

"Why shouldn't I go to camp?" JD100 asked. "I've always been able to go before."

"It's not even his first time!" Robby yelled. "And I've never been at all! Tell him he can't go, Dad."

"He isn't going to camp. This is our house, remember?" Dad whispered while JD moved his duffel bag into the closet.

"You're supposed to stay upstairs in the sunroom. It's a lot nicer there, and you won't have to sleep on the floor," I told him.

"This cabin is exactly like the one I had at a camp on Gallium. I had a very good time there," JD announced.

"He wants to stay in the closet, Dad," I said.

"He can't stay in the closet. My stuff goes in there. I can't leave my things all over the playroom floor. Your mother will kill me."

"Oh? You'll tell him he can't stay in the closet, but you won't tell him he can't go to camp? Don't you see how wrong that is?" Robby yelled. "You have to tell Sal he can't send campers here."

"And how am I supposed to do that?" Dad yelled back.

"What is going on down here?"

Everything stopped for an instant as we turned to find my mother standing at the bottom of the stairs, a guitar case in each hand, her music tucked under her arm. Then, all of a sudden, Dad was insisting that he really did think she meant she wanted him to clean his closet in the cellar and Robby was shouting, "Mom! You've got to let me go to summer camp!" Before I could get a word in edgewise, the three of them were gone and I was turning on our central vacuuming system so I could clean JD's "cabin."

"Is this one of the activities this place offers?" JD asked as he watched a long, thick gob of spider webs disappear up the vacuum's hose.

"It is for me," I complained. "I just started having to help with the vacuuming this year."

"What's so special about you?" he wanted to know.

"I'm the oldest," I sighed. "Vacuuming, mowing the lawn, putting suntan lotion on your mother's back when you go to the lake . . . the oldest child always gets stuck doing those things."

"Hmmm. And how does a camper get to be the oldest child? Is there a test you have to take?"

"It's an accident of birth, like having extra teeth, or two different colored eyes, or no hair," I told him.

I was afraid I'd offended JD, since he was quite bald, but he just nodded his head as if he understood me perfectly.

At dinner JD told us that his mother had heard that Earth was one of those planets that often had problems with lice, so she had given him a camp haircut.

"Shaved your head, did she?" Dad said pleasantly.

"She shaved all of me."

That gave us all something to think about while we ate, and we were pretty quiet until Mom asked JD how long he was staying. That led to another long silence while he seemed to be counting on his fingers. His mouth moved as if he were working out calculations in his head. Then he asked for something to write on. He filled two sides of an eight and half by eleven sheet of paper with little squiggles and then used up some of the margin space.

Finally, when we were ready to leave the table, he looked up from his work and said, "Seven of your days. More or less. I think. Seven days of fun. When does it start?"

"Good question," Rob muttered as he took his dirty dishes out to the kitchen.

"Do you have to be an oldest child to do what he's doing or can anyone try?" JD asked, watching Rob.

Mom let him clear his place, then told him he could go out to play with Robby while I helped clean up in the kitchen.

"Will this be fun?" he asked as he followed Rob out the door.

Robby got a kickball game going on the front lawn with the O. kids and a brother and sister who were riding their bikes out in front of the house. That ended in a brawl, so maybe JD was right when he said it wasn't fun. After I finished loading the dishwasher, we went out to the creek in back of our house and threw rocks in the water. JD thought it might be too complicated an entertainment for him, and said it might be more fun to do something simpler. So then we punched some holes in the lids of old mayonnaise jars and explained that when it got dark enough we would catch lightning bugs and keep them in the bottles.

"I guess that means the fun starts tomorrow," JD said.

After breakfast the next day, Mom told JD that he was going to pick out pieces of construction paper from the pile she was giving him and punch holes in them so he could make himself a book to paste different kinds of leaves in.

"I thought it would be a nice souvenir of your trip to Earth," she concluded.

"What are the other campers doing?" JD asked glumly.

"They're making their beds, picking up their rooms, and making sure their towels are hung up in the bathroom. Then they'll go outdoors with you, and you can start collecting leaves while they do some weeding in the garden."

JD perked up a bit. "Weeding?"

"Don't worry. There's not much to do. It won't be long before they're able to have fun, too."

"We didn't call this fun at any of the other camps I've been to," JD complained when Robby and I joined him. He was sitting on the floor of our deck, pasting leaves onto the pages of his construction paper book.

"We don't call it fun here, either," Rob said. He stretched out on the deck next to JD. "Brendan is going to camp this year," he sighed. "He's going to go swimming every day and make a rocket and learn to use a bow and arrow and sleep out at night and . . . Hey! What are you doing?"

JD had the scissors my mother had given him to cut the stems off his leaves and was using them to trim the grass along the edge of the deck.

"This grass is all different lengths," he said as he got up on his hands and knees and began to crawl along the deck, clipping as he went. "Hadn't you noticed that?"

I had, actually. Trimming the grass along the deck was

one of Robby's jobs, and anybody could tell it had been a couple of weeks since he'd done it. JD took care of the whole thing. Then he noticed that there was tall grass all along the foundation of the house, the edge of the garden, where the lawn met the driveway . . . any place I couldn't get to with the lawn mower. He squealed with delight and took off with the scissors.

He also collected all our lost baseballs, the plastic cups we'd left out on the lawn, and a soggy mitten that Tom had been looking for since February.

"What are the activities for this afternoon?" he asked after lunch.

"Well," Mom replied, "Will and Robby have to clean one thing in their rooms each day this summer, and I thought they'd do that after lunch. Will is going to clean his desk drawers and Rob is going to do under his bed. But you, JD, are welcome to play a computer game."

JD looked at Rob. "There's something under your bed?"

There were tubs of Tinker Toys, Legos, and a Mr. Potato Head under there along with some pajama bottoms Rob had outgrown and half a carob Easter bunny. JD washed and dried the tubs and repacked them. The largest Tinker Toys went on the bottom, the smallest on the top. The Legos he sorted by color. He said Mr. Potato Head looked a lot like a counselor at one of his other camps, and put him up on a shelf where Mr. Head could keep an eye on things. He put the pajama bottoms in the wash so they could be cleaned before being given to the Salvation Army. He ate the carob bunny.

Robby was running downstairs to use the computer when JD came into my room where I'd been sitting at my desk for the last half hour.

"I understand that being a superior older child means that you have the privilege of cleaning your desk drawers yourself," he said, "but could I just watch?"

I had emptied my drawers onto the floor, the first step in cleaning anything. The rest of the time I spent struggling with the question of what to do next. I looked down at all the broken crayons, pencil stubs, and spilled glitter by my feet and said, "You know, I think maybe there *is* a test you can take to become an oldest child."

JD got the vacuum hose (which reminded him of a life form that had become extinct on his home world) and used a special attachment I didn't even know we had to clean out the bits of broken lead, eraser shavings, and crayon wrappers from all the nooks and corners of my desk. I left to go to the bathroom, and when I got back he was rapidly dropping pencils, pens, rulers, rocks, and the odd arm or leg from some old action figures into neat little piles in my drawers.

"I hope you don't mind," he said. "This was my favorite class at camp last year."

"You're company," I said, "so I'll let it go this time."

Then he looked longingly at my closet—*into* my closet, actually, since I couldn't close the door.

"May I?" he asked.

"Well . . . I guess so," I said, trying not to sound too eager.

He went in and, after a couple of tries, got the door to shut behind him. Almost immediately there was a thud, then another. Then came some groans and grunts and a series of knocks, whacks, and bops that brought Robby back up from the play room.

"Is that JD doing that?" he asked, staring with horror at the closet door, which was shaking with each crash. "Shouldn't we get him out of there?"

He was interrupted by a clanging sound that had to be someone tangling with my coat hangers.

"We should find Mom and get *her* to get him out of there," Rob said.

"Not until he's done," I objected.

When he came out, he sighed and said, "If only I could have done as good a job at Camp Dueling Stars, I would have won camper of the week. But, no, Myczar Tunirsee got it just because he put air freshener in the shoes."

"Maybe I shouldn't go to camp," Rob whispered to me as we admired JD's work.

After dinner, we went out to the garage and JD found all our sleds, snow tubes, and skis and took them out to our storage shed. He also sharpened the blade on the lawnmower.

He was up early the next morning to alphabetize the books in Rob's room. That afternoon he painted our walls using odds and ends of paint we found in the garage and a method he'd learned in an arts and crafts class on Palladium 2. Mom thought it was stunning. You could tell by the look on her face when she saw the finished job.

"Come on, guys," Dad said after he got home and was inspecting our rooms. "Don't you think you're taking advantage of JD?"

"Taking advantage of *him*? He's the one who wants to clean all *our* stuff," I replied.

"Besides, he never wants to do anything, Dad," Rob told him. "We offered to shoot hoops with him out in the driveway. He put the ball through the basket once and said, 'What's next?' "

What was next was the attic. We woke up the next morning to the sound of our old tricycles rolling over our heads. JD thought it would be more orderly for them to be stored on the other side of the house. Rob and I ran up in our pajamas to play Attic Wars around our old high chair, playpen, and crib while JD made parking garages out of empty boxes for the trucks we didn't use any more. He even sorted Mom's and Dad's old tax forms.

At breakfast Dad announced that he thought JD should have some fun. "We should all be embarrassed to have a guest doing so much for us."

"Why?" I wanted to know.

Dad ignored me. "What would you like to do, JD?"

JD thought a moment. "Well, the drain has been running slowly in the bathroom. I bet there's some hair in there I'd like to get a look at. And the windows in your sunroom, they look as if they haven't been washed in years. That would be a few hours of fun."

Mom's always telling us that we shouldn't shout out the first thing that comes into our heads. I could tell there was something she wanted to shout out about those dirty sunroom windows. (After all, washing those windows is *her* job.) Instead, she sort of gritted her teeth and said, "Why don't I take everyone to the lake?"

The way she said it didn't make going to the lake sound all that terrific. But I thought it had to beat pulling hair out of a drain. JD asked what we would do when we got there.

"Swim," Robby told him. "Dig holes in the sand. Catch minnows. Play volleyball."

Just listing things off like that didn't sound as great as it should have, either. Still, I wanted to avoid pulling that hair out of the bathroom drain, so I tried to sound enthusiastic.

"It will take us *hours* to get ready, JD," I promised. "We'll have to collect all our pails and shovels and they should probably be washed. Polished even. Then we'll have to find our minnow nets, and I know Rob's has a hole in it—"

"Oh, no, it doesn't," Robby broke in. "*Yours* is the one with the hole."

". . . that has to be mended," I continued. "We have to look for our beach sandals, get the sunscreen, make sure everybody has towels, and find Mom's sand chair."

"And we have to have food," Robby added. "And our big Thermos. And—"

"I think the camp director should provide a certificate for anyone who completes this activity," JD cut in.

"This is going to be so much fun," Rob told him as he watched JD wash and dry our sand toys. "The last time I was at the lake, I dug a hole in the sand so deep a little kid got in it and couldn't get out."

"You dug a hole in dirt? Wasn't it . . . dirty?" JD asked.

While he made us peanut butter and jelly sandwiches, I told him about how Tom and I were allowed to leave the part of the beach that had a sandy bottom and go look for snails in the weeds. "You've got to be careful not to bring any home, though," I explained. "If you leave one in a bucket and forget about it, it will stink something awful."

"So what do you do with them?" JD asked.

"We put them back in the water," I said.

"So what's the point of looking for them in the first place?"

"It's fun!"

We told him about hunting for things at the bottom of the lake and the swimming instructors who gave us candy. We explained about the ice cream truck that came and parked under the trees and how our mother always let us buy ice cream there because the ice cream you get out of the back of a truck at the beach is so different from ice cream you get anywhere else. We promised to play volleyball with him and to show him the best tree in our entire town for climbing.

Everything was ready, the car was loaded, we had our bathing suits on, the house was locked . . . and JD began to cry.

"I want my mother!"

I had one foot in the car already. Mom was putting the key in the ignition. Robby was all buckled up and ready to go.

"This place is too strange! I'm homesick!"

He felt a lot better after he pulled the hair out of the drain in the bathroom.

That afternoon, he restrung the clothesline and told Mom she really ought to buy some stain because the deck looked awful.

"What are we going to do with him tomorrow?" Mom asked that evening while JD cleaned the inside of the tank behind the toilet.

"He could vacuum," I offered.

"Vacuuming is your job," Mom objected.

"But I'd let him do it just this once, Mom. It would be good for me to share."

"Have him clean your car, Reg . . . and the garage," Dad said.

"Would it be really awful for me to ask him to clean out that stuff that collects under the vegetable drawers in the refrigerator?" Mom wondered.

"He'd love it," Rob said.

"You think he could reseed that spot on the lawn?" Dad asked.

JD reseeded the *whole* lawn. He cleaned the entire refrigerator and took care of the freezer while he was at it. He vacuumed the house . . . floors, ceilings, and walls. He flipped the mattresses on all the beds and washed and ironed all the drapes. He cleaned under the bathroom sink. He wallpapered the closet under the cellar stairs with the pages he'd made for his book on Earth leaves, and, just before he left, he moved all Dad's junk back in there.

And, of course, he washed the sunroom windows.

"Gee, it seems as if you just got here," I said on his last morning with us.

"Time sure flies when you're having fun," he agreed. "I'm going to recommend this place to all my friends."

"You promise?" Rob asked.

He hadn't lifted a finger the entire time JD was with us. Not that Rob does much, anyway.

"Oh, yes," JD said. "I had a very good time while I was here."

And so did we.

4
Battle for the Home Planet

There is an old Earth saying about how a watched pot never boils. It means that things you want to happen never will so long as you're waiting for them. This explains why those scientists who spend their lives listening to sounds from space hoping an alien will speak to them are wasting their time and why Rob and I had to clean our own rooms the rest of the summer. Nothing happens if you want it to.

No space guys came anywhere near our place until a day in September when Robby, Dad, and I were supposed to leave for the Sons and Daughters of the Pioneers annual encampment. It is the most important Pioneer event of the year, and I'm not just saying that because I belong to the coolest Pioneer colony in our town.

The Sons and Daughters of the Pioneers is supposed to be an organization for fathers and their children to learn about the early history of our fine country by studying how colonists lived. Like that's going to happen. Dad says it really exists for women who want to get their husbands and kids out of the house for a few hours each month.

"Sounds like history to me," Mom says whenever we come home and tell her the dads took us ice skating or to Chuck E. Cheese. She also says, "I don't care where you go so long as you go."

She particularly likes us to go to the Pioneer encampment. So do we. It's forty-eight mother-free hours of junk food, dirty clothes, and peeing in the woods. No one tells us to brush our teeth. No one tells us to eat with a fork. No one tells us to use shampoo when we wash our hair. No one tells us to wash our hair, for that matter. If the dads would just leave their daughters home, it would be two perfect days.

Nobody knows for certain what Mom does while we're away at the encampment, although we're sure it's stuff we wouldn't be caught dead doing anyway. So Rob and I didn't even ask where she was going when she left with Aunt Connie. We just waved good-bye and went back to loading our cooler of hot dogs and bacon into the back of Dad's station wagon.

We were discussing who was going to get to sleep in our spare tent, Tom and me or Rob and one of his friends, and I was just to about to remind Dad that I *am* the oldest, when we were interrupted by a voice coming from out in the driveway.

"Excuse me," it said. "I believe I have a reservation."

My life flashed before my eyes. At least, my life at Pioneer encampments did. The marshmallow torches . . . the Saturday night banquets . . . the water balloons . . . the fathers keeping us up late while they sang and danced around the campfire pretending to be old rock singers . . .

I could have done without that last part, actually. But otherwise I loved the Pioneer encampments, every minute of them. And as soon as I heard that word—"reservation"—I knew my weekend was in danger, grave danger.

"The name is Corell Wlglicqand Merqhors. The corell is just an honorary title now. I'm retired."

"Retired from what?" Rob asked in a tone of voice that pretty much expressed how all three of us felt about having company just then. "Boy Scouts?"

"The Armada of Her Most Resplendent Excellence, Panzee, The Supreme Director of Bromine and Noble Protectress of the Curium Colonies and—"

"Is that anything like Boy Scouts?" Rob broke in, though, really, this Corell person didn't look old enough to have made it to Tenderfoot, let alone through the whole Boy Scout program.

Dad didn't wait for an answer. He had chipped in fifteen dollars for a pig the fathers in our colony were planning to roast Saturday night, and he had two dozen ears of corn crammed in to every spot he'd been able to find in the back of the car. He didn't want to throw away his investment to spend the weekend with a stranger from a strange land who he would never see again. As cool as aliens were, Dad had seen three of them since January. And this year, there was only going to be one annual Pioneer encampment.

"We're on our way out so you're welcome to make yourself at home in the house," he said. "We get cable, of course, and we've got a remote control for the CD player so you should be pretty comfortable."

Corell Merqhors looked into the car. "Leaving on maneuvers? It's been a long time, of course, but I think I recall a thing or two about moving an army from one place to another."

We decided that this guy wouldn't be the weirdest guest who had been at a Pioneers encampment (that would be Chris Hooperman's Uncle Charles who believed dead presidents talked to him on the telephone), and forty minutes later we were all on our way to the campground. The wagon was so full we'd had to fold down the back seat, which meant there was no place for a fourth life form to sit. We packed Corell Merqhors in the storage area between the tent and a cast iron frying pan, which wasn't as awful as it might sound because seat belt laws really only apply to humans. And since his only complaint was that a being of his status ought to be riding on the hood, we felt that the travel situation was pretty well under control.

"It's a good thing we have this little wagon," Dad said after we got to the campground and were squeezing in between two sports-utility vehicles big enough to live in. "This is the last parking space near our colony, and we wouldn't have been able to take it if we were driving one of these monsters on either side of us."

"You wouldn't have been able to fit into this nice little crater, either," Corell Merqhors pointed out after our back axle dropped into a ditch so deep the front end of the car appeared ready to take off into space.

Tom O. ran over and greeted us with a mighty burp. We burped back, and a few guys who just happened to be walking by burped in passing. Then somebody's dad, who was unloading a truck a few vehicles over, burped and another dad shouted, "That's nothing!" and let out a roar.

By that time, the corell had climbed out a back window.

"I'm glad we got here in time for roll call," he said as the last of the belching was drowned out by a boom box. Then he asked what Dad was doing.

"He's taping the mirror back onto the car," I explained. "It must have dropped off when we hit that hole. He carries duct tape with him everywhere he goes in case something like that happens. In a lot of places it's all that's holding his car together."

Corell Merqhors took the roll of duct tape from my father and studied it. Then he shook his head and sighed sadly. "If they'd had this at the Battle of Gloomzbaltkin, it would have changed the course of history."

"Battle of Gloomzbaltkin?" Tom repeated, mispronouncing the last word.

"He's in some organization like the Boy Scouts," I explained quickly, "but different. I think he's talking about a merit badge."

We introduced Tom to Corell Merqhors and told him that he was going to be staying with us for the weekend.

"Corell? That's a strange name," Tom said.

"It's a title, actually," Corell Merqhors told him. "A military rank, higher than a blastnode but lower than—"

"I know what you mean," Tom assured him. "My cousin is a Scout."

"Oh-oh," Robby warned. "Watch out. Here comes Katie and some of the other Salems."

"Geez," I said. "We haven't even put up our tents. Hey!" I called when they had almost reached us. "Let's pretend we're *really* living in Colonial times, and girls have to do all the housework. Since we don't have a house, you can unload our car for us."

"We're not touching your car. We're here to get our name," Katie explained.

"You have a name—Salem, as in witches," Robby replied.

"You know what name we want," Katie told us. "It should be ours. You have no right to it."

We knew what name they wanted, and we had every right to it. Roanoke. It's the name all the Pioneers want because the colonists at the original colony mysteriously disappeared. Disappearing sure beats raising corn and tobacco, which is all the other colonists did. Our Pioneer colony inherited the name fair and square when we joined the organization in first grade. It came from a colony of older boys who had to give it up when they were thrown out of the Pioneers for making corn whisky at a Colonial Cooking Festival. The Salems were out of their minds if they thought they were men enough to take our name from us.

"This is your last chance," Katie warned. "Hand it over."

"Never," I said.

"This means war," Katie promised as she and her friends turned and walked away.

"War?" Corell Merqhors asked.

"Ah, don't worry about it. They declare war every year at the beginning of the encampment," Robby explained.

"Except for that year when we did it," Tom reminded him.

"And who wins?" Merqhors asked, sounding very interested.

Robby snorted. "We do, of course. Sort of."

"It's not a war that anyone actually wins," I said.

Corell Merqhors smiled. "We'll have to do something about that."

According to the corell, the first thing an army needed to do was establish its position, which meant unloading the car and setting up our tents. Evidently, establishing positions is something corells don't have to do since he sat on the front seat of the car and listened to the tape player while the rest of us worked. When we were done, he told us we would have to select a guard to protect our base while we surveyed the enemy's location.

"Dad will guard our base," I promised. He and a couple of the other fathers from our colony were busy deciding where they wanted their lawn chairs to go. Then they would have to decide who was going to go out for pizza, where he would go, and what he would get. They would be busy for a long time.

We put together a scouting party made up of Tom, Rob, Corell Merqhors, a couple of other guys with nothing to do, and myself and headed over to the Salem colony's tents, which just happened to be located right next to ours. We hid between two vans and crept up close enough to see a group of girls huddled around a campfire while two others set a picnic table with paper plates and cups.

"I can't believe it," Tom snorted. "They're setting the table for supper. They're actually going to *sit down* to eat. What a bunch of girls."

"What are the people near the fire doing?" Corell Merqhors asked.

"Playing with Barbies," I explained.

"Is that some kind of weapon?"

"If the girls get mad enough, they'll throw them at us," I said.

"I got hit on the back of the head with a Barbie once. It left an awful mark," Rob added.

"Watch this," Tom said. He stood up, took a small ball from his pocket, and threw it into the Salem campsite. It bounced once and hit Katie's friend, Tiffany, in the center of her back.

"We're under attack!" someone shouted over the victim's screams.

"There they are!" Katie yelled, pointing at us. "Get 'em!"

"Excellent use of the element of surprise," Corell Merqhors told Tom as we scrambled out from between the vans.

"Run! Run!" I shouted as I pushed him ahead of me.

We tore around parked vehicles, past tents, and through other colonies' campsites.

"Hey!" my father yelled after us as we raced through ours. "What do you guys want on your pizza?"

The chase continued, with the girls running after us most of the time, though there were a few minutes when we took off after them, until the Salem colony was called for dinner. By that time, the rest of our own colony was already squatting around an open fire with pizza so we joined them.

"This food isn't quite what I was led to expect," Corell Merqhors said after he had eaten some pizza.

Rob leaned over and whispered to him, "That's because whenever we've had 'company' like 'you,' they had to eat my mother's cooking." He straightened up and spoke in a more normal voice. "This is *much* better than what we get at home. Mom puts scary things like eggplant on pizza. Here, try a piece with salami, pepperoni, and sausage. It's the best."

The corell sniffed at a pepperoni. "Are you sure this is safe to eat?"

"Pepperoni is always safe," I explained. "It's preserved so well it'll last forever."

"What is it, exactly?" he asked.

Robby shrugged. "Who knows? Who cares?"

The corell ate a couple more pieces and said, "I don't feel quite right."

"If somebody's going to blow chow, make sure you do it out in the woods," one of the dads called from the picnic table where they were all playing cards and trying to scare each other with stories about hard drives crashing.

"Have some Pepsi," Tom suggested. He handed Corell Merqhors a liter bottle so he could take a slug. "Pepsi Cola will always cure what ails you."

Merqhors took a sip and choked. "Are you certain?" he gasped.

"Sure. It'll make you burp, and you'll feel better."

Corell Merqhors held his nose and brought the bottle back up to his mouth.

"Our Aunt Connie says that pigeons can't pass gas so you can't ever give them Pepsi because they'll explode," Rob said. "Aunt Connie is a nurse and knows lots of disgusting stuff."

Corell Merqhors pulled the bottle away from his mouth and seemed worried. But it wasn't long before he started rumbling and sure enough a long wail of a burp came moaning out of him.

"Oh. I do feel better," he said, sounding surprised.

We finished off all the pizza and went through a box of Twinkies, three bags of cheese puffs, and four more bottles of soda. After it got dark, we started sneaking around to all the girls' colonies and when we came upon a tent that looked as if there were girls in it sleeping, we got up close and belched. If someone yelled at us or sounded as if they were coming out of the tent, we took off to another colony. If no one yelled or moved, we figured they hadn't heard us and we just belched louder. Tom and I taught Corell Merqhors to burp out that song about the monkey who wrapped his tail around a flagpole. We sounded great until Merqhors started throwing up. Then we decided it was time to go to bed.

Merqhors said it would be bad for discipline for a corell to sleep with someone of lesser rank and insisted on taking our spare tent for himself. This meant Dad,

Robby, and I had to cram into a two-person tent. I would much rather have slept with an alien, but he wouldn't have me.

"What is that horrible smell?" Corell Merqhors groaned the next morning as he crawled out of his tent.

"Bacon," Robby said as he tipped his head back and dangled a stiff, brown strip over his head for a second before letting the whole thing drop into his mouth.

The corell clapped a hand over his mouth and ran out into the woods.

When he came back, we were sitting at the picnic table sucking the juice out of the last few strips of the three pounds of bacon cooked to perfection by a couple of the fathers. He collapsed at one end of a bench and asked for some Pepsi.

"So what are you going to do this morning?" Tom asked.

"I don't know," I said. "What are you going to do?"

"I don't know."

"What are the girls doing?" Rob asked.

"Good question," Merqhors groaned. "You should always know what the enemy is up to. Didn't you post sentries along your colony's borders to keep guard over night?"

"Ah . . . Well, I had to sleep over in their colony with my sister and father," Tom said.

"A spy! That's even better. And what did you find out?"

"Nothing."

We finally just looked over into the Salem colony and watched until we saw the girls leaving. Then we followed them to the campground's pond.

"Hmm," Corell said. "It looks as if they're laying land mines along the harbor."

"Land mines? They're making sand sculptures. I love doing that," I said, and I took a step forward so I could go down to the beach to join them.

Corell Merqhors grabbed my arm. "You're not going over to the enemy are you?"

"Just for a while."

"I'm going, too," Tom announced.

"You do recall that we're at war, don't you?" Merqhors demanded.

He sounded as if we'd better recall it.

"It's not a *real* war," I started to say, but the Corell cut me off.

"There is only *one* kind of war," he declared.

"Cool," Robby said. "Can I be a general?"

Since no one else wanted to do it, the position was his. Once he had the title, he forced Tom and me to retreat to the top of the little hill that overlooked the pond. He and Corell Merqhors kept us there in the hot sun while they formed a battle plan.

"We're not going to do that," I complained when they told us we were going to attack the girls on the beach. "It's not nice."

"This is war, Will! Nobody worries about being nice in a war," Robby said.

"We'll need more troops," Merqhors decided. He looked at Tom and me. "And better ones, too. Perhaps we should order a draft."

Tom and I were ordered to hold our positions, which meant sitting at the top of the hill for fifteen minutes and watching the girls have a good time without us, while Robby and Merqhors went off to search for able-bodied citizens to draft into their army. They didn't have much luck.

"Everybody's afraid they'll get in trouble for fighting," Robby explained when they got back.

"You are a planet of cowards," Corell Merqhors sneered.

"Who *is* this guy?" Tom asked as Robby led a charge down the hill toward the beach.

Tom and I took our time getting there. By the time we arrived, Robby was on his knees in the sand trying to rebuild the mermaid whose head he had just kicked off and begging two small girls to stop crying. Katie and Tiffany were guarding their sand sculpture.

"Touch our turtle, and I'll tell Mom when we get home," Kate warned us.

"That was the most pathetic excuse for a battle I've ever seen in my life," Corell said as we headed back to the campsite for lunch. "They did absolutely nothing, and they still beat us."

"Don't worry," I promised. "We'll get them after we eat."

"Oh, no," Corell moaned. "It's time to eat again?"

Early in the afternoon we snuck off to the old clay pit that bordered the campground where we had a couple of hours of peace making mud bombs.

"They're going to be really, really mad when they find out about this," I assured Corell.

"I should think so. Look at the incredible pile of weapons we have to use against them."

"Actually, we're just going to throw these against the walls of the clay pit. We're not allowed to take them back to the campsites, because the fathers don't like having to clean clay off the tents. No, what will make the girls mad is knowing they missed out on all this fun. You just wait and see," I said.

"You guys are filthy. Where have you been?" Tiffany asked when we got back.

"Oh, we were just at the clay pit. Did you want to go, too?" I asked, really sounding as if I cared.

"Are you kidding? We found a place where you can dig up garnets," Katie exclaimed and she held up a paper cup full of the little stones.

"Jewels!" Rob cried. "Where did you get them?"

"We're not telling. We found them. They're ours," another girl told him.

"If you found the garnets here on the campground, then everyone can go there," I pointed out. "You have to share."

"You have to share the Roanoke name, but you don't. We're not sharing the garnets," Katie announced.

"We can't share a name!"

Katie just shrugged at me. "Find a way."

"They don't seem very upset," Corell said as the girls walked away to plan the jewelry they were going to make out of their garnets.

"We should have brought the clay bombs back," Robby grumbled.

"We'll get them tonight," I said.

"That's what you said before," Corell pointed out.

"This time it's a sure thing. In a few hours it'll be Saturday night. That's the night we have the big competition to see which colony can make the best dinner."

Robby nodded his head. "Nobody's going to beat us Roanokes this year."

We waited a little while so that the girls wouldn't think we were too interested. Then we pretended to just run into them as we were walking around.

"Gee, hasn't your colony started your dinner yet?" I asked.

"It's only three o'clock," Tiffany said.

"Our fathers started our dinner right after lunch."

Two of the girls laughed as if starting dinner so early just meant our dads were really lame or something. But I could tell by the look on Katie's face that she knew what I was driving at. She couldn't help it. Her brother was a Roanoke, and her father was in both his kids' colonies.

"Darn it!" she exclaimed, stamping her foot. "They're roasting a pig!"

"And what is it I heard you guys are having?" Robby asked innocently. "*Just* spaghetti . . . again?"

"It's not *just* spaghetti. We've got green salad with croutons and homemade garlic bread, too," someone said.

"Like anybody eats green salad and garlic bread," Rob laughed.

All the girls oohed and aahed and made a big fuss over us because roasting a pig really is quite cool. For the next couple of hours the Roanokes ruled that campground while the Salems, and everyone else, kept coming by our colony and asking to look in the old file cabinet one of the Roanoke dads had rigged up with a spit to roast the pig on. And when we weren't receiving our adoring fans, we were piled in the back of a Winnebago watching videotapes on one of the other dad's VCR and TV.

It was pretty close to dinner time when we came out. The pig and the corn and potatoes that were roasting with it were nearly done, and I was explaining to Corell that we had definitely won this battle. Roast pig was . . . well, it was roast pig and no one was going to come up with anything as good as that. I was looking down at the spit when I realized something was wrong. Our pig, which had been ordered from some dad's friend of a friend and had arrived in a garbage bag, had never looked exactly like Porky. But after six hours of toasting it was looking even less pig-like.

"Hey!" I exclaimed. "Where's its head?"

"I think we overcooked it a little," Mr. O. said. "It dropped off the spit. You can't do anything with it, so when Katie and Tiffany asked if they could have it, I said yes."

"They've got our pig head!" Robby cried.

Corell Merqhors made a fist and said, "The line must be drawn *here*."

We didn't have a clue what he was talking about—no one wanted to draw anything—but he sounded mad so when he took off for the Salem colony, a crowd of Roanokes were right behind him. When we got there, we were confronted with a horrible sight. Our pig head had been jammed onto the end of a stick and was being displayed next to their camp fire for all to see. Worse yet, Katie and Tiffany were decorating it with hair ribbons.

"Hand over our pig head, and no one will get hurt," the corell ordered.

"It's our pig head," Tiffany insisted. "Katie's dad said we could have it."

"He didn't know we wanted it," I explained.

"Like we want the Roanoke name?" Katie asked. "Roanoke should be a girls' colony name, not a boy's, because Virginia Dare was born there. And she was a girl."

"Ah, being born is no big accomplishment," Robby complained.

"Well, neither is being a dead pig," Katie declared,

and she started to stick a barrette through one of our pig's ears.

"We're putting an end to this *right now,*" Corell Merqhors announced. "We want our pig head back or we are going to destroy your entire civilization. There will be nothing left but ashes when we're through with you. The destruction will be so fast and so thorough you will never know . . ."

He suddenly broke off and pointed toward their picnic table. "What's that over there?"

Tiffany looked suspicious but said, "A green salad."

"With croutons," someone added.

Corell Merqhors ran toward it. "May I have some? I haven't been able to keep any food down since I got here."

"Forget the salad!" Robby shouted. "Get our pig!"

We charged toward the pig head, but Katie and Tiffany stood their ground and were joined by other Salems. I thought Tom had the stick the head was stuck on once, but his sister beat him back. Then I got hold of the pig's snout, but it slipped out of my hand. Finally, Robby had one of its ears, and I thought the head was ours. But then Tiffany grabbed the other ear and . . .

Well, I guess Mr. O. was right and the pig was overcooked because the next thing we knew his head was nothing but a pile of bones and gristle on the ground. And suddenly I found myself feeling a lot more generous.

"You can have it," I told Katie.

I dodged two Barbies before making it back to the safety of our own colony.

Mr. O. made Merqhors come back to our spare tent to sleep that night, but otherwise the corell spent the rest of the encampment with the Salems.

"It looks to me as if they're winning," he explained as he ate a couple of the girls' apples and watched us load the car to go home. "And since I don't have the slightest idea what you're fighting about, I thought, why side with losers?"

"We still have our name," I insisted.

"That's nice." He threw an apple core out into the woods. "You'll have to excuse me for a while. I promised Tiffany I'd braid her hair before we leave."

"Oh, yuck, he's braiding hair?" Rob groaned. "No human guy would be caught dead doing that."

I saw Kate loading sleeping bags into the back of her family's mini-van.

"You just wait until next year, Katie!" I warned her.

She tipped her head at me and smiled. "Next year," she promised.

5
Alien Abduction

The Sons and Daughters of the Pioneers encampment is the first sure sign of autumn. The second is the arrival of the school fundraisers. There is "fun" in "fundraiser." All the grown-ups who run them say so.

"Look, Mom!" I said as I tried to run across our front lawn one afternoon a couple of weeks after the encampment. I had two cardboard boxes in addition to my backpack, so it wasn't easy getting into the house, even though Mom had met us at the door and was holding it open.

"Show me later, honey. We've got . . . "

I dropped the boxes at her feet. "Look what they gave us at school."

"I got something, too," Robby broke in. He had turned his backpack upside down and dumped all his things on the entryway floor so he could dig through them.

"I'm sorry, Rob. It's going to have to wait."

"It can't wait," Robby insisted as he continued to root around. "Ah! There it is."

"Come with me," Mom said and she hurried us through the kitchen. Then she whispered, "We have a problem."

"I knew you'd say that," Robby complained. "Every other kid in the fourth grade is going to make hundreds, maybe THOUSANDS, of dollars. But not me. I'm never allowed to do *anything*."

Mom stopped at the entrance to the dining room. "I'd like you to meet my sons, Will and Rob Denis," she said to someone who was in there. "Boys, please say hello to Grubb Vogel and Polek Pogie."

I stuck my head through the door into the dining room again and took a look. There, seated next to each other at our table were two . . . well, on our planet they'd be called women. Women with hair that strange brown/blonde/white color my great-aunt's gets when she's been dyeing it too much. And thin blue sweaters with something like buttons down the front. And lime green pants with wide legs covering the bottom halves of their bodies.

"How do you do?" I said politely.

They looked us over, their lips slightly parted, their bodies leaning eagerly across the table. One clasped her hands and said, "What lovely specimens!"

The other smiled and said, "Wouldn't I just love to have one of those for my very own!"

Mom pulled Rob and me back into the kitchen.

"So why can't I sell—"

"Would you forget about whatever it is you're selling?" Mom hissed at Rob. "I start jury duty tomorrow. Who's going to watch those two while I'm gone?"

I shrugged. "Why does someone need to watch them? Even Grandma Judy would think they're old. What are you afraid they're going to do? Cheat at bingo?"

Mom flashed one of those "I'm-not-in-a-good-mood" smiles and said, "When I found them they were out in No Mom's Land trying to stuff one of Tommy O.'s little brothers into a sack."

"It was all a terrible misunderstanding," the woman named Ms. Vogel explained as she walked across the dining room and got close to me—real close.

Ms. Pogie came up next to her and bent down a little so we were almost nose to nose. "We just wanted to pick up a little souvenir," she said as she studied my eyeballs. "We would have paid. You do understand buying and selling on this planet, don't you?"

"When I travel I buy those little magnets in the shape of states," Robby said from where he was standing behind them. "You ought to see if you can find some of those."

"Close your eyes, Polie," Ms. Vogel ordered, and they both immediately closed their eyes. They were so close to me I would have felt their lashes on my cheek—if they'd had any. "Now open them."

Their eyes popped open. Their irises were a pale violet color that I suppose could occur in nature, and they jiggled all around their eye sockets as they gave me the once-over again.

"Does he look any different to you, Polie?" Ms. Vogel asked.

Ms. Pogie shook her head. "Not a bit. Maybe we should make a note of that."

She hurried over to the table and reached into a big leather shoulder bag that was lying on it. She took out what looked like a pad of order forms, but instead of writing on it, she spoke to it.

"Subject has not changed in three and a half minutes."

"Hey!" Robby said suddenly. "Would either of you like to buy some gift wrap? The fourth grade at my school is selling it to raise money for a new playscape. If I sell thirty dollars worth, I'll win a pencil." He waved the catalog he'd found in the things he'd dumped on the floor. "I have samples."

"And you're going to try to meet your sales goal and

win that marvelous incentive, are you?" Ms. Vogel asked. "Good for you!"

"That's how we got here!" Ms. Pogie exclaimed. "Our company offered this trip to Club Earth as an incentive package to the sales team that made the most sales last quarter."

"It's the third trip we've won in the last eight fleeckles," Ms. Vogel added.

They sounded like potential customers to me, so I started waving my own catalog as well as my two order forms that needed to be filled out in duplicate. "I'm selling sweatshirts for the school band. And I have two boxes of candy bars to sell to raise money for our class trip."

Ms. Pogie flipped through Rob's sample catalogue. "You've got your work cut out for you if you hope to win that pencil. I like to think I can sell anything, but this stuff . . . I can't even tell what it is."

"But it's for a good cause," I explained.

Ms. Vogel and Ms. Pogie looked at each other and chuckled.

"You couldn't use that sales pitch on a developed world," Ms. Vogel explained. "You'd be laughed off the planet."

"Can you believe it?" Rob said later while Mom was making dinner. She had stationed us in the sunroom to keep an eye on Ms. Vogel and Ms. Pogie who had gone back outside. "They can get everything we're selling cheaper from their own distributor."

"No, I can't believe it," I replied as we watched Ms. Vogel and Ms. Pogie race through the woods trying to catch a squirrel to put in one of those big handbags they carried with them. "They didn't even know what gift wrap is. They just told us that distributor story because they didn't want to buy anything. We can probably forget about Dad coughing up money for more than a candy bar, too. When he looked in his checkbook and yelled, 'I'll tell that band director what he can do with his sweatshirts!' I knew we were out of luck."

"And Mom says she can't even talk about the fundraisers until she's through with this jury duty thing. Why do grown-ups make such a big deal about jury duty?" Rob asked. "All they have to do is sit in a courthouse with a bunch of other people listening to strangers argue all day and then vote for the one they like best. I wish somebody would ask me to do that."

Rob was right—grown-ups do make a big deal about jury duty. Why, even as Robby and I were speaking about it, we could hear Dad out in the kitchen trying to say, "Three fundraisers? They have *three* fundraisers? All at once?" while Mom just interrupted him to shout, "I have jury duty tomorrow! Jury duty! The boys can't stay home alone with those two after school! What are we going to do?"

"I don't know. We just don't have enough relatives to cover *three* fundraisers," Dad replied.

At dinner Ms. Vogel told us that, with a sound marketing strategy, a good sales person could move any product. "What is yours?" she asked Robby. She stared at him intently.

He just stared back.

"Your plan for selling your merchandise," Ms. Vogel explained, speaking very slowly as if that would help Robby to understand her. "You do have one, don't you?"

"Oh! Of course. I'm going to go up to people, look real cute, and say 'Please, please, please, buy something from me.' "

Ms. Pogie rolled her eyes. "Don't they teach you anything in your schools? Why, by the time I was your age I was expected to be able to come up with three different ways to sell any item my teacher handed to me. And only then was I allowed to engage in commerce. I can't believe your species turns its untrained young loose with sales forms."

"Neither can I," Dad muttered.

"Speaking of our young," Mom said, trying to sound very casual, "I thought we should discuss this business of grabbing them and stuffing them into bags. You can't do that on this planet, no matter how much you're willing to pay."

"Too bad," Ms. Pogie replied. "That would make one *terrific* fundraiser."

"Your adults are too big," Ms. Vogel complained. "We'd never be able to sneak one through customs, and if we declared it, we'd have to let the customs officers quarantine it for six months. Who needs that kind of aggravation?"

Ms. Pogie started to pout. "I suppose you're going to tell us those gray things that seem to live in trees are off limits, too. You have so many of them. Surely you could spare just one?"

"Squirrels? We could spare a dozen," Dad agreed. "And we'd let you have them for nothing. But you'll never catch one."

"What . . . what would you do with it if you did?" I asked hesitantly.

Ms. Vogel turned her attention to me. She hardly even blinked as she said, "Watch it. That's our hobby—watching life forms evolve."

"You mean you watch species change? Doesn't that take a long time?" I asked. I could have added, "Like millions of years?"

"Oh, we have plenty of time," Ms. Pogie replied. "We're on vacation."

"You see," Ms. Vogel said, her eyes scanning my face, "we travel a lot, being in sales as we are. We needed a hobby that didn't involve a lot of equipment the way, say, creating different forms of energy does . . ."

"You need a reactor for that," Ms. Pogie broke in. "Besides, it's a geeky past time."

". . . and we hit upon watching different types of life forms evolve. We see enough of them in our line of work. It's so easy. You don't even have to take notes, if you don't want to, and you meet lots of nice folks at the Galactic Natural History Conferences."

"We're a fun bunch!" Ms. Pogie agreed.

"If you wanted a hobby that didn't involve having to carry a lot of things with you, why did you want one of the O. kids?" I asked.

"If we could have done an in-depth study of just one of your life forms and written a little paper on it, why, we could have had it published in a professional journal," Ms. Vogel said. "We would have made quite a name for ourselves in the scientific community."

"Maybe it's just not meant to be," Ms. Pogie sighed, looking longingly at Robby.

Mom insisted that Dad stay home from work the next day while she put in her first day of jury duty. She said she would try to convince the judge to replace her with someone else.

"Would you take one of my boxes of candy bars with you?" I asked. "Maybe you could sell some to the other jurors."

I thought it was the least she could do after making me stay home after dinner to study for a social studies test instead of going out to do a little business.

The couch in the sunroom was only big enough for one person, so Mom and Dad had to give up their bed to Ms. Vogel and Ms. Pogie. Mom made Dad sleep in a sleeping bag outside their door to act as a guard while she slept in the sunroom. The next morning all they did was complain about the awful night they'd had, and we were glad to leave for school just to get away from them.

When we got home, Dad was sacked out on the couch with the springs Lard Butt had ruined while Ms. Vogel and Ms. Pogie watched him.

"Dad, Dad," Robby said, shaking his shoulder. "Can we go sell stuff this afternoon? Tommy and Katie have already been to a whole bunch of places. If we don't hurry, they'll get to everybody before we do."

"And Katie's selling Girl Scout Cookies, too," I added. "Pretty soon nobody's going to have any money left."

"Don't leave the street by yourselves," Dad muttered as he rolled over. "Not safe . . ."

Mom wasn't home. Dad was sleeping. Who were we going to go with?

We heard Ms. Vogel laughing behind us. "These two are going to try to sell something," she said to Ms. Pogie. "I'd like to see that."

"Okay," I agreed.

We loaded up with our stuff, and the four of us headed out.

The street was crawling with people. There were kids out with parents, grandparents, older brothers and sisters, baby-sitters, or the family dog. They were hauling order forms, samples, and sometimes cases of merchandise. They were racing each other from one driveway to the next and sometimes up the driveway to the front door.

Ms. Vogel's head swung from side to side as she tried to watch everyone we passed. "Are these all your competitors? There are an awful lot of them."

"Maybe we could rent one for a little while," Ms. Pogie suggested. "We could study him, and you could have his sales territory until we brought him back. We'd pay a deposit, too."

"We better take turns going up to doors," I whispered to Robby. "Mom's right. These two shouldn't be left alone for even a minute."

Robby agreed immediately. Then he said that he should go first.

"Why?" I asked.

"Because you've sold things for fundraisers before. This is my first time."

"Come on. You sold chocolate bunnies at Easter last year so your class could go to a zoo," I reminded Rob.

"Doesn't count. Mom bought them all."

"Oh, if you've never sold to the public before you better let your brother go first," Ms. Vogel told Robby. "Watch everything he does. Salesmanship requires careful training."

"I don't want people watching me," I objected.

"Give me that," Ms. Pogie said impatiently. She grabbed my sweatshirt catalogue out of my hand and took off up the path to a house.

"Oh-oh. You never send an adult to a door for a kids' fundraiser," I warned.

"Wherever did you get that idea?" Ms. Vogel asked.

"All the kids know that. Grown-ups aren't cute. They're only good for selling things where they work."

"Just watch Polie," Ms. Vogel assured him. "She'll show you how it's done."

Before we got a chance to get close enough to see how it was done, it *was* done. Ms. Pogie was back with an order, paid in full.

"They don't have to pay until delivery," I said as I pocketed the money.

"What kind of system is that?" Ms. Pogie demanded.

"Always . . . *always* . . . ask for payment up front," Ms. Vogel instructed us. "That's how it's done on all your more advanced worlds."

Then she gasped. "Polie! Look at that girl over there. I just saw something move near her right hand. I think she's growing a sixth finger."

At the next place we tried, Robby came back to the street and said the woman who answered the door had told him she had all the gift wrap she could use.

"Then go back and try again," Ms. Pogie ordered.

"But she said no," Robby reminded her.

"Never take no for an answer," Ms. Vogel said.

Rob said he'd do that at the next house he tried.

When it was my turn to try a house, no one answered the door.

"You left a card with your name and number, of course," Ms. Vogel said to me.

"I don't have any cards with my name and number."

Ms. Pogie grumbled something that included the word hopeless.

Robby was gone a long time at his next house—refusing to take no for an answer, as it turned out. Finally, we heard a woman yelling, "FOR THE LAST TIME—I SAID NO, AND I MEAN NO!" and Robby came running back to the street, his catalogue of samples flapping against his leg.

"I want to go home!" he howled.

"You're never going to win that prize staying at home," Ms. Vogel warned him.

"It's only a pencil. I don't want it anymore," Rob said.

Ms. Pogie said she knew Robby didn't really mean that, and she and Ms. Vogel dragged us the length of three streets. They told us to believe in our candy bars and gift wrap, to know without doubt that owning one of our school band's sweatshirts would make life better for every person who had eighteen dollars to pay for one, and to pound on every front door we passed.

Rob and I sold two packages of gift wrap and four candy bars, which Ms. Vogel and Ms. Pogie said just wasn't good enough.

"They can put me in a bag and take me anywhere they want so long as I don't have to push any more doorbells," Rob moaned to me as Ms. Vogel tried to shove him toward another house.

We finally got home just before my mother came staggering into the kitchen, her blouse falling out of her skirt, her blazer jacket dragging on the floor.

"Well, I tried," she sighed as she opened the refrigerator and took out a casserole that had stunk up the kitchen every time the fridge door opened all day. "I told the judge I needed to be excused from jury duty because I had two guests."

"You didn't think she was going to let you off for that, did you?" Dad asked. He had jumped off the couch when he heard Mom's car coming into the garage, and he was trying to smooth down his hair without her noticing that he had been sleeping on the job.

"I told her my guests were from another planet—I didn't know which one—and that they needed to be watched constantly because they wanted to abduct a human so they could watch it evolve—"

"They said they'd pay," Rob broke in.

"Buying and selling human beings is against the law on this planet, so I thought it was better not to bring it up. I did mention the paper they wanted to write and the Galactic Natural History Conference, though."

"Geez, Mom," I said. "You weren't supposed to tell anyone about the aliens."

Mom tossed the casserole into the oven and slammed the door shut. "I hoped the judge would think I was crazy and dismiss me. But all she said was that people use the 'alien' excuse all the time to get out of jury duty and that I should think of something more original. I couldn't have been more embarrassed if she *had* thought I was nuts."

All the time she was talking, Mom was moving around the kitchen, getting out a salad bowl, some lettuce, a couple of tomatoes. When she opened a drawer and pulled out a chef's knife, we didn't think anything of it. Then, suddenly, she was in the living room where Ms. Vogel and Ms. Pogie were watching The Home Shopping Network.

She pulled Ms. Vogel off her chair, held the knife to her throat, and said, "If you take one of my children—if you take any child—I'll hunt you down. If you can get to my planet, there's a way for me to get to yours. I'll never rest 'til I find it. You'll never be safe. Do you understand me?"

"Get a load of Mom, Will!" Rob exclaimed. "She's just like Xena the Warrior Princess!"

She *was* pretty cool there for a few minutes. Then things got kind of hectic. Dad had his hand around one of Mom's wrists so he could try to get the knife away from Ms. Vogel's throat, and Rob and I were pulling at the other one to try to make her let go of the sweater. In the meantime, Ms. Pogie was shouting, "How many times do I have to tell you, we weren't going to *take* anything! We were going to pay! We weren't stealing! We were shopping!"

"Where did you think you were?" my mother shouted. "The mall?"

The mall?

"Dad," I said. "I have an idea."

Rob and I rushed to get our homework done while Dad finished making dinner, Mom took a long bath, and Ms. Vogel and Ms. Pogie studied mail-order catalogues. After dinner, Mom listened to music and let Ms. Vogel and Ms. Pogie stare at her while we guys ran an errand.

When we got back, Mom said she'd talked to Aunt Connie on the phone and that she'd agreed to buy something from both Rob and me. "Of course, in exchange I had to buy fifteen dollars worth of cheese from your cousin Brendan. His school is selling it to raise money for a computer lab."

If we'd had time, I would have asked if she knew how much cheese they had to sell at Branden's school to buy a computer lab. But I didn't. Rob was trying to grab the carton I was holding.

"Be careful!" I ordered. "You'll ruin everything."

"Mom! Will's being greedy again," Rob said as he elbowed me in the gut and tried to pry my fingers from the package.

I managed to get the box open, but it was Rob who exclaimed, "Here's a little souvenir of your trip to Earth. Even with its cage, it's small enough to fit in one of your handbags. You're so lucky. Dad wouldn't get anything like this for me."

Ms. Vogel and Ms. Pogie looked into the box.

"What a tiny specimen," Ms. Vogel said.

"And it's ours? For our very own?" Ms. Pogie asked.

"It" was a mouse, one of the cheap ones you get at pet stores for feeding to snakes. It was the youngest one we could find, because we thought Ms. Vogel and Ms. Pogie would get a kick out of watching it grow—a mouse fate that had to beat ending up as a reptile's lunch.

"This is perfect, just perfect," Ms. Vogel kept saying as we helped them move their specimen into its cage and gave it some food and water. "Wait 'til we show up at the Galactic Natural History Conference with this."

"I have friends who are going to be so jealous," Ms. Pogie told us. "I can't wait. Let's leave tomorrow, Grubbie."

"But you know what we should do first? We should take care of the rest of these boys' sales for them. They'll never do it on their own."

"That's for sure," Ms. Pogie agreed as she experimented with hiding the mouse cage in her handbag. "Earth people know nothing about the fine art of salesmanship."

"Do you remember those six houses we went to today where no one answered when you went to the door?" Ms. Vogel asked us. "Well, there was someone home at four of them. They were hiding inside. I could feel them in there. We would never let a buyer get away with that."

"What could we do? We can't make people come to the door," I said.

"We can," Ms. Pogie bragged.

"Get us your samples and merchandise. We'll get rid of it before we go to bed. Then we can get an early start for home tomorrow."

"But it's getting late," Mom objected as Dad told us to run and get our order forms and candy bars before Mom had a chance to change their minds.

"That's the very best time to try to sell someone something," Ms. Pogie said as she slid our order forms into her purse and lifted up one of my boxes of candy. "If I can get hold of a tired buyer, I can make a sale."

"Evolution may be our hobby," Ms. Vogel said as she headed out the door, "but sales, that's our life."

It was so quiet in the living room in the moments after they left that you could hear a pin drop. So, of course, we had no problem hearing Dad's car starting out in the driveway.

"They're taking my wagon," he cried as he ran to try to stop them.

"Mom?" Rob asked. "Can I have a hamster?"

We were in bed when the station wagon rumbled into the driveway and started to rattle and shake next to the garage. A crash out in the yard brought me right out of my bed. My whole family was out in the driveway before Ms. Pogie and Ms. Vogel could get out of the car.

Or what was left of it.

Not that it looked as if it had actually been damaged. There was no sign that it had hit anything or rolled over. But one door was off altogether, and another wouldn't close properly. The headlights looked as if they had been shaken loose. The back seat was no longer attached to the floor. One of the long windows along-side the storage area was just gone. There wasn't a sliver of glass anywhere. It was as if the whole window had just popped out somewhere. The muffler was dragging on the ground. From the looks of it, it had been dragging for a while. A fine red powder, like a red shadow, covered the driveway under the car. The rust that had been clinging to the fenders and underside of the car had dropped off along with a few bigger, more important looking things.

Ms. Vogel and Ms. Pogie led us back to the living room where they emptied their purses of dollar bills and order forms.

"We didn't have anywhere near enough of those things you call candy bars," Ms. Vogel said as she handed me a stack of cash. "Next time you should plan to stock up on at least twice as many. We found lots of people around here eager to buy."

"One person told us he'd buy anything we wanted if we'd just go away. You don't find easy sales like that on most worlds," Ms. Pogie declared.

"We could have taken a lot more orders," Ms. Vogel explained. "But we were afraid that vehicle of yours wouldn't last even the eighty miles we needed to go to get back here. So we had to quit early."

"You went a hundred and sixty miles in two and a half hours and made stops to sell things, too?" Dad asked. "That explains a lot."

"If you hope to be successful in sales, you're going to have to find yourself a better method of transportation," Ms. Pogie complained as she picked up her new mouse cage and began to stare at its occupant. "The one you've got is falling apart."

"Get rid of it," Ms. Vogel advised before she went to bed. "Replace it with one of those sports utility vehicles. If I were working on this planet, that's what I would get. I've heard you can go anywhere with one of those things."

6
An Alien Threat

You love your parents because they're your parents, and you love your brother because your parents say you have to. There's a logical explanation for it. There was a logical explanation for why Dad loved his station wagon, too. It was because it was paid for. Except for duct tape and gas, he hardly ever had to spend any money on it. But all the cash in the world (this one, anyway) couldn't fix what Ms. Vogel and Ms. Pogie did to that old car on its last ride. As for the second hand sports utility vehicle we replaced it with? Dad said he'd be paying for it for the rest of his life. Things would never be the same.

Mom couldn't have been happier. Not only were Ms. Vogel and Ms. Pogie gone, but so was Dad's station wagon. And if Mom had to start substitute teaching a couple of times a week to help pay for the new truck? Well, the only thing my substitute teachers ever do is yell, and complain, and refuse to let anyone do anything at recess. That kind of thing is a cinch for Mom. She was so pleased with the way things turned out that after she got her first paycheck, she took us to the mall to buy Rob a hamster.

"It sure is a good thing those fish we had died. Where would I have put Chip if we didn't have these empty aquariums?" Rob asked one afternoon when Mom had gone directly from a school where she was working to the grocery store.

"You could have fed him to the O.'s cat," I suggested.

I had used my key for the first time to let us into the house after we got off the bus. I had been waiting for months to do that. I finally got my chance, and for what? So I could sit in the playroom and listen to Rob yak on and on about his Siberian dwarf hamster. Siberian dwarf hamster—that's just a fancy name for rodent. And rodent—that's just a fancy name for rat.

"I'm going to save that money Aunt Connie and Grandma Judy gave me for my birthday for one of those plastic cages with tubes and an exercise wheel. You'll like that, won't you, Chippy?" Robby cooed. He was holding an incredibly tiny, silky-looking ball in one hand and stroking it with the other. Its little body stretched every time Rob's finger ran along its back.

"Look how soft he is. Did you notice how he already lets me pick him up whenever I want? Did you, Will?"

I noticed.

Robby made a big show of looking into the other aquarium.

"You really chose a good name for your hamster, Will. Chewie. That's perfect for him."

"He's named for Chewbacca in *Star Wars*," I told him.

"Oh. I thought you named him Chewie because he bites."

No, it was just dumb luck the way that turned out.

I hadn't even wanted a lousy hamster. It was all Robby's idea. But when we got to the pet store and Mom was buying R*ob* a hamster, and buying R*ob* a water bottle, and buying R*ob* pine bedding for his aquarium, and buying R*ob* all-natural hamster and gerbil feed . . . Well, one thing led to another and I ended up with one of those incredibly tiny, silky-looking balls, too.

When I got him home, he started gnawing through my finger.

Siberian dwarf hamster—that's just a fancy name for rodent. And rodent—that's just a fancy name for rat.

Chewie had buried himself under a pile of pine chips so I couldn't even look at him and I sure wasn't interested in watching Robby and Chip, so I headed upstairs. That's why I was the first to notice the noise in our backyard.

"Hey, Rob!" I shouted after I'd enjoyed the scene from a sunroom window for a while. "Come see this!"

"It better be good!" Robby complained after he came up from the cellar. "I have important things to do, you . . . What is going on out there?"

It was hard to say. But, basically, someone was pounding on the door of the little shed in our yard and shouting, "Hello, in there!" to our lawn mower and baseball bats. Every now and then he'd stop and look over his shoulder. A few times he flattened his back against the side of the shed and crept to the edge so he could look around the corner. Once he looked up to see a squirrel over his head flip from one branch to another. That started him yelling, and he dropped to one knee with his arms over his head.

"This is just great," I said. "The very first time we're alone in the house an alien comes. What are we going to do? Mom and Dad said we can't even let our friends in when we're by ourselves. I can just imagine what they'd say if they came home and found an alien in the living room."

Our newest arrival grabbed the handle to the shed door and began pulling on it and yelling, "Now! I've got to get in there now!"

"If we don't do something soon, Mom and Dad are

going to come home and find all the neighbors in the yard," Rob said.

I opened the back door and shouted, "What's wrong?"

The stranger jumped and stared at me for a moment. Then he said, "Wrong? Whatever makes you think something is wrong?"

He covered his face with his hands and raced across the yard to our deck. Which gave me just enough time to lock the screen door so we could talk without letting him in.

"I didn't realize this was the registration area. You should mark it better," he said, peering out from between his fingers at me. "Well, your brochure says this is a retreat for carbon-based life forms who enjoy getting away from it all and I'm a carbon-based life form. Show me to a room."

"There'll be a slight delay," I said, wondering how much grocery shopping Mom planned to do. "Why don't you have a seat in one of the lawn chairs? Someone will be with you in a little while."

"I can't wait," he whispered.

"Why?" Rob asked. "Do you have to use the bathroom?"

"Robby!" I objected.

"He's come a long way," Robby said.

"It may not be safe out here," the alien explained.

"Sure it is. Nothing *ever* happens in our yard," Rob told him.

"You can't be too careful. Not in my line of work," the alien said as he slowly brought his hands down and tried to look through the windows of our house. "Being careful has got me through more than a few star systems, I can tell you that."

"What's your line of work?" I asked.

He looked over his shoulder again and then leaned against our screen door. "I'm with Interpol—the Interstellar Police," he said in a low voice.

"That is *so* cool," Robby exclaimed.

The alien smiled modestly. Then his eyes opened wide with what looked like terror to me, and he stared wildly at Robby's hands.

"Drop it!" he yelled. "Drop it fast and stamp on it! You'll only get one chance! If you miss, run for your life!"

Then he turned and ran for *his*. He got as far as the end of the deck where he caught sight of a couple of chipmunks playing tag on the lawn. He turned around and raced back to the house.

"Your planet is being overrun! Quick! You must have some kind of weapons here! We can at least try to fight . . ."

Robby held up his cupped hands so he could show the new alien what he was holding in them. "It's a hamster," he said. "You're afraid of a hamster? Are you sure you're some kind of space cop?"

"A *ham*ster?" the space cop repeated. "Is that some kind of little pig?"

"What?" Robby howled. "You're calling my little Chip a pig?"

It sounded good to me.

"Look, kids—you are kids, aren't you?—I'm going to tell you the truth. All our lives may depend on it. I'm an officer with the Interstellar Police, and the most dangerous assassin in the universe is after me. Now, let me in so we can secure this shelter you live in."

"If you're with the Interstellar Police, why are you wearing a shirt that says 'Tri-Planetary Bar and Grill'?" I asked.

The alien looked embarrassed. "I've just been working there undercover. I'm not *really* a cook."

"So I guess your name isn't really Alphonse like it says on your shirt, either," I said.

"Of course not. I just told you. I've been working there undercover. You don't expect me to give my real name if I'm working undercover, do you?"

No. But then I didn't expect him to tell me *any* of this stuff if he was working undercover.

"We'll let you know when your room is ready," I promised.

It was the beginning of November, and all "Alphonse" was wearing was a T-shirt and a pair of shorts (it must have been hot in that kitchen he worked in) so I did feel a little sorry for him huddled in one of our cold, metal lawn chairs. But all the time he was waiting, he was shouting things in to us about how we would regret how we'd treated him after he'd been torn to bits before our very eyes and how his species' blood stained badly so we'd have it on our lawn furniture forever. I finally shut myself in my room and started my homework so I wouldn't have to listen to him.

My father drove into the yard right after my mother arrived with her load of groceries, so they met our new guest together.

"He doesn't *really* work at the Tri-Planetary Bar and Grill," I explained with a big wink. "He's really an agent with the Interstellar Police."

"I used to be an agent with a special crime unit. You know—TWA, the Trans Worlds Agency? But those days are behind me now," Alphonse said sadly.

"I see," Dad replied as Mom loaded him up with bags of green, leafy things she planned to force us to eat.

"And he claims his name isn't really Alphonse like it says on his shirt," Robby added. "But who would choose to be called Alphonse?"

"I *love* that name," Alphonse objected. "My mother was named Alphonse."

"Just a moment," Mom called after Robby, who was trying to sneak into the house behind Dad. "Where do you think you're going?"

"I think I'm going inside," Rob said.

"Not without a bag, you aren't. Here, carry something into the kitchen," Mom ordered.

"Oh, Mom," I complained as Rob and I each took a bag before heading into the house. "We shouldn't have to help with this. We were at school all day."

"So was I," Mom said as she took the last bag and closed up the car.

"But you're a teacher. You don't have to work while you're there the way we do," Rob told her.

"Maybe you could go grocery shopping on days when you're not substitute teaching," I suggested. "Then you could take care of everything while we're not here."

"That's a very good idea he has there," Alphonse said to Mom.

She shoved her bag at him, and said, "I've got a better one. You carry this into the house. Will and Robby will show you where to put it."

"I can't believe it," Alphonse grumbled. "I, the agent who infiltrated the More Minerals Mining Company on Molybdenum, have now been lowered to acting as a lowly pack animal."

"I know how you feel," I told him.

"Oh, do you really? Have you ever prevented a planet from having its gravitational pull changed? Have you? I didn't think so. Those miners were going to remove illegal amounts of ore from that planet. Changing a planet's mass by strip-mining so there's less gravity is not pretty, let me tell you. Once a planet's gravitational pull changes, the resident species can't live there any more. More Minerals was planning to buy up property cheap from homeowners who would then have to leave and sell it for a bundle to life forms that don't need much in the way of a planetary draw. Oh, it was an evil plan. And they would have carried it out, too, if it weren't for me. I saved a whole world. And now look at me. I'm a . . . a . . ."

"A cook at the Tri-Planetary Bar and Grill?" I suggested.

Alphonse corrected me. "An undercover cook," he said.

Mom got a call the next morning from a school offering her two days of work. She took it, believing that any alien who had spent most of the night peering out under window blinds so he could cry out a warning whenever a squirrel or chipmunk got too close to the house was no threat to the preschoolers on our street.

We beat her home that afternoon. As soon as my key turned in the door, we heard the central vacuum system start. Alphonse had found the hose and figured out how to hook it to the power source in the wall. We found him down on one knee in the hallway that led from the kitchen to our bedrooms. He had connected the long skinny attachment for cleaning corners to the hose and had it propped between his chin and one of his shoulders like some kind of rocket launcher while the vacuum's motor roared down in the cellar.

"You don't have to do that," Rob told him. "It's Will's job."

Alphonse looked surprised. "You're the security guard here?"

"Hardly," I said as I pulled the other end of the hose out of the wall, turning the central motor off. "I have to help clean the floors. Now that Mom's working part time, I sometimes have to vacuum the whole house."

Alphonse looked at the hose in amazement. "Vacuum?" he said.

"I wish I could vacuum," Rob complained. "It's no work at all with the central vac. All those little pipes in the wall carry the garbage down to the can in the cellar. It's like vacuuming the starship Enterprise or something."

I looked at Robby and shook my head sadly. "That's what I used to think when I was your age."

"You didn't happen to see anything unusual on your way in, did you?" Alphonse casually asked as he got to his feet.

He had helped himself to one of my father's pajama tops, which he was wearing with Mom's long denim skirt. In the waist band he'd stuck an impressive looking hammer he'd made out of Rob's old Tinker Toys. Had we seen anything more unusual than that? No, we had not.

"I was thinking of something black and white and fluffy."

"That's the O.'s cat," I told him.

"It's just a pet, Alphonse," Rob told him. "Like Chip."

Rob meant to be reassuring, but as we all headed down to the playroom to see the pets there, I could hear Alphonse behind me muttering about spies. And when he saw Chewie, he pulled his Tinker Toy hammer from the waist of Mom's skirt, started waving it in the air, and shouted, "Look! Look! There are two of them now! Soon there'll be dozens of them! We have to kill them before they take over the house!"

Rob knocked Alphonse's hammer out of his hand. It hit the floor and fell apart. Great, I thought. Another mess for someone to clean up.

"Cut it out, Alphonse," Robby ordered. "You're going to scare my little Chip."

Rob pulled his hamster out of its cage and started cooing into its ear. "Don't worry, Chipper, we won't let the big bad alien hurt you." Then Rob rubbed his cheek against the Chipster's back, and the Chipster rubbed back, and it was all so nice and sweet that I wanted to puke.

"Be careful with that thing," Alphonse warned. "There are hundreds of cute, furry, little species like that one in this universe. They'd all just as soon rip out your guts as look at you. It's because they don't need a whole lot to live on, so they overpopulate their habitats. When there's too many of them, they get hungry. And when they get hungry, they get mean. They'll attack anything, and they'll do it for money. They work cheap, too. All they want is enough to keep them in seeds and grain. You wait . . ."

"Our hamsters didn't come from an overpopulated habitat," I broke in as I moved toward Chewie's cage. "They came from a pet store at the mall."

Chewie took one look at me and raced to the far corner, sending bits of pine bedding flying in all directions as he tore through it. Before I could even get the lid off the aquarium, he was backed against the glass and hissing at me.

"What did I tell you? Now you see why they have such an awful reputation," Alphonse said.

He should have been worried about his own reputation, which wasn't in very good shape after Robby saw his bedroom.

"What have you been doing in here?" he wailed at Alphonse.

Alphonse looked at the tubs of Tinker Toys and Legos that had been pulled out from under Rob's bed and dumped on the floor. He shrugged innocently. "I just did a quick inspection. It wasn't very thorough, I'm afraid. There are so many places for things to hide here, I just couldn't get to all of them."

He'd been thorough enough. The little cupboard filled with comic books and action figures was nearly empty. The contents of every one of Rob's desk drawers were spread on top of his bed. The books and magazines from his bookshelf had been dumped on the floor. Mr. Potato Head appeared to have had some kind of breakdown that had caused him to go to pieces. We'd arrived home just in time to keep Alphonse from starting in on Rob's closet.

"It's a darn good thing I did this, too, because I found evidence of alien life," Alphonse said. He gingerly held up the miniature Paddington Bear that Grandma Judy had brought Rob from England when he was little. Paddy was still wearing his little blue jacket and even his black plastic boots. But his insides were spilling out of a slit that ran from his chest to his crotch. I think he'd been what books call "disemboweled."

Robby started to howl, and I shouted, "What did you do that for?"

"Well, I didn't know he was already dead," Alphonse explained, defensively. "You're darn lucky he died of natural causes before he was able to carry out his mission. I mean, look at the size of this fella. He would have done a lot of damage."

"You're the one who did a lot of damage!" Rob screamed while I hurried across the hall to my room.

Alphonse followed me. "I'm sorry I didn't have a chance to even get started over here. I'll—"

I blocked my door with my body. "That's okay," I quickly assured him. "I'll inspect it."

"Are you sure you know what to look for?"

I didn't have a clue what to look for, which didn't matter because I wasn't planning to do anything with my room other than keep Alphonse out of it.

Later that night, Alphonse found me down in the playroom trying to coax Chewie into sniffing my fingers. Mom had convinced Alphonse to give her back her skirt, and he was now wearing a pair of Dad's sweat pants. He looked a lot less creepy, even though he'd had to roll up four or five inches of the legs so he didn't fall over them.

"Ah-ha! I'm glad to see you're taking my warning seriously and are keeping a watchful eye on that murderous butcher. Though I wouldn't put my hand in there if I were you. He's fully capable of ripping it right off your arm," Alphonse said to me

"He's never even broken my skin when he's bitten me," I said sadly. "I just wish he liked me."

"Those things don't like anybody. Don't let it bother you."

"Robby's hamster likes him."

"It's all a trick," Alphonse assured me. "That creature's just biding his time. When the right moment comes, he'll attack."

I sighed. "Maybe I made a mistake getting Chewie."

"Of course, you did. You ought to get rid of him."

"Give him away?" I asked.

"You could eat him," Alphonse suggested.

"Gross!"

"On some planets the ruling species eat them."

"Not here," I told him. Then I said, "I don't want to get rid of Chewie. Out of all the Siberian dwarf hamsters in that pet store, I chose him. He was for me. I just wish I could do things with him."

"The kinds of things that creature does, you don't want to do," Alphonse insisted.

I went to bed feeling kind of down and didn't sleep very well. During one of the few times I did manage to doze off, I woke up to find Robby standing on my bed.

"There's something here," he said.

"Me," I groaned.

"I heard something moving in my room," Rob insisted. "It woke me up, and it followed me in here."

I sat up. "Where is it?"

"I don't know. I didn't see it, I heard it."

We were both quiet and listened.

"I don't hear anything."

"It must be hiding now," Rob explained.

"Robby, you had a bad dream because Alphonse ripped Paddington Bear's guts out and tore your room apart."

"Mom!" Robby shouted from the foot of my bed. "There's something in Will's room! Come quick!"

It only took a few hours for everybody to get back to sleep after hearing that.

Fortunately, the next day was Saturday, when most of the world kicks back, watches hours of television, shops for pointless computer games, and takes part in organized sports. Of course, Saturday morning is when Robby and I have to clean our rooms.

"I hope you're going to tell me that that thing hanging from your bed post is *not* the mummified remains of a vicious, man-eating beast," Alphonse said nervously. He was sitting in my chair, with his feet up on my desk, thumbing through the TV *Guide*.

"Alphonse!" Robby shouted from his own room across the hall. "Get over here and help me!"

Before Mom took off to pick up our father, who had

broken down with the sports utility vehicle, she had suggested that Alphonse give Rob a hand cleaning up his room.

"Actually," I said, "it's Squeaky Monkey. My father brought it to the hospital to give to me when I was born."

Alphonse rolled his eyes. "He gave a dried monkey to a newborn child? You are a very strange people."

"Alphonse!" Robby yelled again. "You made this mess . . ."

"Okay, okay," Alphonse said as he got up. "But I want to vacuum."

Since Alphonse had never had an opportunity to be alone in my room, it was nowhere near as dirty as Rob's. All I had left to do was to kick my bathrobe and a couple of shirts into the back of my closet when I suddenly had this feeling that I was not alone. Something, I thought, had scooted along the floor under the jackets and pants hanging from my clothes bar. I looked, and I looked again. But all I could see was one of those woolly boogers that grow up from dust in places where parents don't look much.

It was particularly large, of course. And it had teeth.

I hadn't been screaming long when Alphonse tore into my room, armed once again with the vacuum hose.

"At last we meet!" he shouted as he raced into my closet. Over the sound of the vacuum I could just make out some growling and spitting.

"Don't worry," Alphonse said to Robby and me when he came back out, looking pleased with himself. "Nothing can survive being vaporized."

"Maybe not," I agreed. "But all you did was vacuum that thing up."

"Meaning what?"

"Meaning now it's somewhere in the vacuum pipes that run through the walls and under the floor."

"No!" Alphonse dropped the hose and started kicking holes in the wall. "We've got to find it!"

"You can't do that. There are pipes all over the place. It could be anywhere," I told him.

"No, it couldn't," Rob said. He turned the vacuum off. "Listen."

Loud and clear we could hear something banging against metal in the cellar.

"It's in the can where all the dirt collects," Rob said. "I've got to get down there before it gets out and attacks Chip!"

By the time we got downstairs, "it" had kicked a hole in the side of the vacuum canister enabling it to escape, along with a cloud of dust that was slowly filling the cellar. I picked up an empty clothes basket from the laundry room, hoping to use it as a trap, and Rob got Dad's old electric guitar from the closet under the stairs for use as a weapon. Alphonse had dragged the vacuum hose into the cellar with him, though it was of even less use now that the vacuum was turned off. We got down low, figuring that's where it would be, and hoped that would give us our best chance to see it before it saw us.

"Be careful," Alphonse whispered. "It could be anywhere down here."

"What is it?" I whispered back.

"Remember the mining company I was involved with when I was a special agent for Interpol?"

"Back before you became a cook? We remember that," I said.

"Well, the owners were on to me."

"And they're here? On our planet?" Robby asked in disbelief.

"No, of course not. The owners are on a penal planet now. All except Nuvo Astra. The arresting officer didn't fill out the arrest form properly so the judge let Nuvo go."

I recalled the sight of Rob's bedroom after Alphonse got through 'inspecting' it. "You were the arresting officer, weren't you," I said.

"Hey, mistakes like that are made *all* the time. You'd have thought Astra would be grateful to me. Instead, she was mad. She swore she'd get me. I had to change my name, give up police work, and move to another galaxy. I had a whole new—and not very pleasant—life as a cook in a café on a farming world. But then she found me."

"So you really were an interstellar police officer," I said in amazement.

"Isn't that what I've been telling you right along?"

"And you sucked up a crime boss in our vacuum cleaner?" Rob asked.

"No, no, no. She's not here. It's her hired goon. It followed me across two galaxies. Stubborn little thing."

We were huddled next to the table where we kept our hamsters' aquariums. "It's close by," Alphonse whispered. "I know it. I can almost feel it breathing down my neck."

My legs were getting cramped, and I had to stand up to stretch them. I carefully got up, looking all around to make sure nothing was going to jump me. When I'd gone around in a full circle, I was looking directly into Chewie's aquarium.

It, whatever it was, had made a hole in the screened top of the aquarium and dropped down next to a pile of sunflower seeds. It was watching me. Slowly, it began to smile. Then it rushed me. I closed my eyes and waited for the sound of glass shattering.

Instead, I heard a terrible scream. When I opened my eyes, I saw two gray forms locked in combat within a storm of pine bedding. The aquarium shook all over as one little body or another was thrown against its sides.

"Don't look, Will," Robby advised as he pulled me away from the scene of the battle. "It's better that you not see."

It was some time after the cellar grew quiet again before we could get up the nerve to approach the aquarium. As I'd feared, only one little gray ball of fluff was left standing. It was huddled at the end of a toilet paper tube, breathing heavily and staring at some fur and toenails at the bottom of the cage.

"Chewie, Chewie," I sobbed. "You saved my life. You like me!"

I started to pull the lid off the aquarium. "We've got to help him. We've got to get him to a vet," I cried.

"Why?" Rob asked. "He doesn't have a mark on him."

"That is one mean little hamster you've got there," Alphonse said appreciatively.

"I know," I said proudly.

7
An Alien Invasion

Grandma Judy likes to say that guests and seafood should leave after three days. She usually likes to say that when we've been visiting her for close to a week. We didn't wait that long to start talking about sending Alphonse back to wherever he came from. By the time he had been with us for forty-eight hours, our house looked as if a riot had been conducted in it.

"It's not my fault," Alphonse insisted when Rob and I blamed him for the big bill my parents were going to have to pay to have a new canister put in for the vacuum cleaner. "I didn't punch my way out of that thing. *It* did."

"But *it* wouldn't have been in the canister if *you* hadn't vacuumed it up," Rob insisted.

"How could I have possibly guessed that a central vacuuming system is for cleaning floors and not vaporizing intruders? You don't find that kind of thing on any other planet that I've been to."

"I told you I cleaned the floor with it," I reminded him.

"Well, I have a vaporizer I dry my clothes with," he said. "I can still protect myself with it if I have to."

"It doesn't matter how it happened. It wouldn't have happened if you weren't here," Mom pointed out. "Hotels can throw out rock stars and athletes when they destroy hotel property. I should be able to throw out an alien."

"I saved your offspring from the most dangerous assassin in the universe. Don't I deserve some credit for that?" Alphonse complained.

"We don't need an interstellar police officer to protect us," I said. "We have Chewie."

"I don't want to go home. I don't like my new life as a cook. I'm on my feet all day, and I'm always getting burned," Alphonse whined. "It's much nicer here."

Dad got up to go to the front door where someone was ringing the bell. "Maybe it would be a good idea to let him stay for a while," he suggested. "All these different aliens marching through here is getting kind of old for me. Maybe so long as he's here, no one else can come. How long was your reservation for?"

"Reservation?" Alphonse repeated as Dad opened the door. "I was on the run. I didn't have time to make a reservation."

We heard Dad gasp, and a noise that, we learned later, was the front door banging against plaster, leaving a hole in another one of our walls. We couldn't actually see what was happening in the entry but we could tell that some sort of mass of energy or force of nature was driving its way into our home. And then, suddenly, it was there in the living room with us.

"Are we being invaded?" Robby cried as he jumped to his feet.

Alphonse shook his head. "Nah. It's a tour group. You can tell by the little tattoos stamped on their foreheads."

Three men paused just long enough to look around the room. Then one of them told us we were "Charming, just charming" while the other two went right over to the television. They sat down in front of it and turned it on. One grabbed the remote and started channel surfing until he found one of those history of flight shows on the Discovery Channel.

"Look, Bru," he said to his companion. "They understand comedy here."

A young girl who had followed them in propped her fists on her hips and stared at us.

"I thought you said there'd be billions of males on this planet, Auntie," she said, sounding disappointed.

"That's what I read in the guidebook," a woman told her as she entered the room.

They had come for Thanksgiving, they said. Evidently, Sal was creating vacation packages designed around Earth holidays. They suggested we should expect a really large group for Christmas.

It took hours to get them all settled in. Miss H'ld'n and her niece, Klair, finally took over Mom's and Dad's room. ("You'll be sorry," Alphonse told Dad. "The two young guys say the aunt's a bed wetter.") Once we convinced them that watching the time change on our clock radios was way more fun than TV, Bru and the third male, Der, agreed to take Rob's and my bedrooms. ("Are you sure you want to leave them alone with your things?" Alphonse asked. "If you ask me, they look like the kind of creatures who will take anything that's not nailed down.") Professor Dorqus was easy to please, declared the sunroom charming, and moved right into it. (Alphonse made a gesture that I suspect is considered pretty rude back where he comes from and shouted, "Charm this, why don't you!" as he watched the Professor take over the couch he, himself, had been using for the last two nights.)

We had to do take out for dinner—sixty dollars worth of stuffed tomatoes and grilled vegetables with corn bread from Beth's Garden Bowl (or Beth's Toilet

Bowl as Robby likes to call it). Professor Dorqus said that take out is a charming eating practice unique to Earth. The others seemed to like it, too. Miss H'ld'n asked if the males of our species cooked, and if they didn't, could they be trained to while Bru and Der said they would very much like to know what kind of equipment Beth used to make foods taste differently.

"Remember that café we were in where everything tasted the same?" Bru asked his companions.

"Which would have been okay if it tasted good," Der said.

Both Bru and Der had lips that curled up like a duck's bill, anyway, and they turned them up still more as they recalled the earlier meal with disgust.

"That was an awful trip. 'A Farm World Excursion'—what were we thinking of?" Miss H'ld'n snorted so hard she made her earlobes, which hung almost to her shoulders, jiggle.

"A café on a farming world?" I repeated, looking at Alphonse.

"Of all the cafés on all the planets in all the galaxies—of which there are fifty billion, more or less, in this universe alone—why do you assume they just happened to be in the one where I was working?" he complained.

"Because they said the food was lousy," I replied. "And if you cook like you do everything else . . ."

Miss H'ld'n reached over and patted Alphonse's hand. "Perhaps it was your day off," she suggested.

She smiled at him, gave his hand a little squeeze, and then held it in her own.

"The male farmers weren't very attractive, either," Klair complained as she opened a small container of what looked like yellow wax and used a little of it to polish one of her own rather large earlobes. "I liked Bismuth better. That's where we saw StarPrance. The lead prancer was wonderful."

"He fell down!" Bru objected.

"It sounds as if you've done a lot of traveling. We never seem to go anywhere. Everyone comes here instead," Mom sighed. She pretended not to notice Alphonse struggling to get away from Miss H'ld'n.

Professor Dorqus smiled at her—I think. His features were so small in his great big head that it was hard to notice them. "You should join our cosmic tour. We never run out of places to go."

"And we meet so many interesting beings. Klair and I have been seeking mates," Miss H'ld'n announced. She smiled fondly at Alphonse who thrashed at the end of her arm like a fish at the end of a line.

Alphonse claimed he couldn't help load the dishwasher after dinner because his hand was too sore. All the time Rob and I worked, he leaned against a counter licking his red fist. He stopped just long enough to inform us that the babes always went for him in a big way.

"I think you ought to go with this one when she leaves," Rob said as he dumped what someone had left on a plate into the trash, leaving a long trail of goo dripping along the side of the basket.

"Nah. As attractive as I find the dear lady's enchanting mustache, I'm a homebody," Alphonse replied as he surveyed *our* kitchen with a happy smile. "I'd never tie the knot with a galaxy-trotter."

I didn't like the way that sounded. "I think she really likes you, Alphonse. How long can this trip she's on take?" I argued.

"Didn't you hear the Professor? They're on a cosmic tour."

"Tours don't last forever," Rob said.

"Cosmic ones do. Well, maybe not forever, just until all the members of the tour group are dead."

Rob and I agreed that that was as good as forever.

"I'll let that school know I can't work Monday," Mom said later that night while we were all settling into our sleeping bags on the floor in the play room.

"You better not," Dad replied. "On Monday we're going to have to pay to get the truck out of the shop. We've got to get the vacuum cleaner fixed and find someone to patch up all the holes in our walls. It cost us sixty dollars to feed this crew tonight, and we've got to keep feeding them right through Thanksgiving. That's twelve days . . ."

"Twelve days!" Alphonse broke in from the closet where we had stashed him for the night. "I can't stand having five extra life forms here for twelve days!"

"And then there'll be more aliens here for Christmas," Dad said, making sure Alphonse heard him. "Reggie, we need to have you working because we're going to need the extra money."

"But we can't leave this group alone and unsupervised," Mom objected. "What if they go out and wander around? There are five of them. Even if they didn't look . . . well . . ."

"As if they came from outer space?" I suggested.

". . . the neighbors would be sure to notice," Mom concluded.

"Will and I can stay home from school when you have to work," Rob offered. "We could take care of everything for you."

Dad seemed interested. But, of course, Mom wasn't buying it.

"What about Alphonse?" I suggested.

"Alphonse!" Mom laughed. "There'll be nothing left to this place if he's in charge."

"He's here anyway," I reminded her. "He refuses to leave."

"Why not put him to work?" Dad agreed.

"Because he's supposed to be a guest here," Alphonse called out of his lair.

We reminded him that since he had never made a reservation for Club Earth, he wasn't actually paying anybody anything to stay with us. He said he shouldn't have to pay anybody anything to stay in a closet. What about the damage he had done to our house? we asked him. What about it? he replied.

"It's too bad you can't slip a few Vanadium beetles under their pillows tonight," Alphonse grumbled after we finally got him to agree to try to keep the aliens in the house. "I guarantee you your problem would be gone by morning. Either your tour group would have cleared out or the beetles would have eaten their heads off."

On Monday we let ourselves into the house after school and found Alphonse stretched out on the living room couch while Professor Dorqus stared at the television. He must have been there for hours because his little eyes seemed so worn out they looked like tiny slits in his vast, doughy head.

"What's that on the TV?" Rob asked.

"It's something on the Argentinean Broadcasting Company's network," Alphonse told him.

"Argentina? We don't get any stations from Argentina," I said.

"We do now. And from Israel, Hong Kong, and northern Canada, too. Just about everywhere. Well, there is a problem with the American stations but you're probably sick of them, anyway. Bru and Der fixed that little box on the television so the Professor could preview Earth's tourist attractions. He wants to take some day trips."

"The cable box?" I repeated. "Nobody's supposed to mess with the cable box."

Professor Dorqus changed the channel. "The Great Wall of China," he said. "Isn't it charming? How do we get there from here?"

I went into the kitchen to try to find something to eat while Rob and the Professor talked about which way you'd turn when you left our street in order to get to Asia.

"Oh, no!" I cried. "What happened in here?"

It looked as if all our dishes, glasses, cooking utensils, and spoons, forks, and knives were spread out on the counters, on top of the stove, in the sink, and even on the floor. There was a trail of them leading into the dining room. And they were all filthy.

"We had to fix ourselves something to eat," Alphonse explained. "Six mammals can't feed without dirtying a few dishes. Look for the salt and pepper shakers while you're cleaning up. I thought I saw Der slip them into his pocket."

Neither Robby nor I had any part of making that mess, so we didn't think we should have to clean it up.

"Then who should do it?" Mom asked when she got home about fifteen minutes after we did.

We didn't say anything. It was so obvious that she should have to do it that we thought she must be asking us some kind of trick question. Maybe if we had tried to reason with her, things would have turned out differently. Instead, after a hard day at school, we had to do the loading-the-dishwasher routine while our mother scrubbed something hard and dry off the stove and washed the counters, walls, and floor.

The next day Bru and Der arranged for us to get a new Internet access provider. It cut us off from everybody on

Earth but made it possible for them to play games online with some friends they'd met while they were visiting the casinos on a desert planet. Professor Dorqus asked when we'd be arranging for them to see some sites. He thought he'd like to get a look at the equator. The bed in my parents' room had to be changed because Ms. H'ld'n wet it. Mom cancelled the guitar lessons she gives on Tuesdays because she was afraid to have her students come to the house. She also had to go to the bank to get money to buy groceries—a hundred and eighty-seven dollars worth. She figured it would be enough to last until after breakfast on Saturday.

"Have you noticed the Professor's head?" Alphonse asked as he followed Robby and me through the house Wednesday night. We had been sent on a mission to find two CD's, some potholders, and the mouse from the computer, which were all missing.

"How could we not notice his head?" I replied.

"Listen to what Klair told me: Dorqus belongs to a species whose members' brains continues to develop and get larger all through their lives. The growth is stimulated by the facts the brain takes in. Eventually Dorqus' brain will get too big for his head and then . . . BANG! His head's going to pop like a balloon!"

Robby was not impressed. "You're making that up."

"Am not. What's more, it gave me an idea. All we have to do is find a way to get enough facts into the professor to make his brain do all its growing right now and . . .

BANG! We have one less alien. Here on Earth do you have something called an encyclopedia?"

We did, but we weren't having any part of giving one to Professor Dorqus. He was too nice a guy to force to read an encyclopedia. Besides, no one in my family would have time to clean up the mess afterward. The dishwasher always needed to be loaded or unloaded. The dining room table always needed to be cleared. The floor always needed to be picked up. If we managed to get everything off the floor, it then needed to be vacuumed. The washing machine and dryer ran all day except for the days when Mom worked. Then they ran all night. There was never time to fold anything. We just hunted through baskets of clean clothes for what we wanted, wore it, then put it back in the wash.

By Thursday night, the tour group had been with us for five days and Thanksgiving was still almost a week away. It took an hour for Mom to clean up after dinner. Then she gathered us together in the play room and told us she had some good news. A music teacher at the elementary school in the next town had fallen off a stage during a rehearsal for the winter concert, she announced.

"That's good news?" Rob asked.

"She's going to need a substitute every day until some time in February. I've been offered the job," Mom exclaimed.

"T*hat's* good news," Dad agreed, hugging her. "A regular income would help a lot right now, Reg."

Mom snuggled against him and said, "With me working full-time we'll need to do a little reorganizing. There's laundry, ironing, shopping, cooking, cleaning, running errands, changing beds, yard work . . . We'll just divide all the chores up among the four of us."

Dad looked at us over Mom's shoulder. His eyes were nearly popping out of his head. He was thinking the same thing Rob and I were.

We were going to do *what*?!

Mom had work lists ready for the three of us when we got up the next morning.

" 'Clean the mirrors in the bathrooms?' " Rob read out loud. " 'Strip my bed on Monday mornings?' 'Collect trash on Dump Day?' I don't want to do any of this."

"I have to clean the toilets," Dad said. "I'll trade with you."

Mom wanted to get to her new job early and she had to drive Dad to work first because his sports utility vehicle had broken down in the driveway, so she just made breakfast for the aliens. We had to make our own. We ate it standing up.

When we got home after school we found Alphonse—worn out, I supposed, from trashing the kitchen again—napping on the couch.

"Where is everyone?" Rob asked.

"They said they were going to the Riviera," Alphonse said without opening his eyes.

"You let them go to the Riviera in France?" I asked.

"If France is in the woods behind your house, yes," Alphonse replied.

Rob and I looked at each other.

"They're down at the creek. I hope they don't get all wet and drip all over the place when they get back," I said.

"This is horrible," Rob moaned as he collapsed onto one of the living room chairs. "I haven't been in my room for almost a week, I'm sleeping on the floor, and I have to help clean up after aliens. I want my mom to come home and fix everything."

"I hope she'll be able to take over making lunch soon," Alphonse said. "Making my own every day is killing me."

"Dream on. She just took a job that's going to last three months. And she's got to keep it. We need the money to feed all the aliens that keep coming through here," I told him. "There's no stopping them."

Alphonse sat up on the couch and stretched. "You know what we need? We need to have an outbreak of Tunella here," he yawned.

"Oh, sure," Robby snapped. "Just like we need some killer beetles or an encyclopedia that will blow someone's head up. Geez, Alphonse, for a guy who used to be a cop you're awfully bloodthirsty."

"Ah, Vanadium beetles are extinct in most galaxies. Everybody knows that. And who could have guessed that on this frontier world you'd have dozens of encyclopedias? But there's no way you can have Tunella here. It's caused by one particular organism that only grows on food stored in the artificial environments of spaceships." Alphonse shook his head. "It's too bad, too. Just rumors of a Tunella epidemic will ruin business in any public establishment that serves food."

"Just rumors?" I asked. "What does it do to you?"

"I've never had it myself, but I've heard it causes your lunch to leave you body the same way it went in."

Rob laughed. "Maybe that's what Corell Merqhors had. Remember how he kept heaving into the woods at the encampment, Will?"

As a matter of fact, I did.

"All we need is a rumor," I said, thinking out loud. "We could manage that."

Alphonse, of course, didn't have a clue what I was talking about. But Robby was beginning to catch on.

"How?" he asked.

"We're going to need quite a bit of money and a way to get to the grocery store."

Alphonse reminded me that Dad's utility vehicle was out by the house.

"But it doesn't work. And even if it did, no one can drive it," Rob pointed out.

"Bru and Der are handy boys," Alphonse said as he got up off the couch. "I'll get them to take a look at that truck."

"How much money did Grandma Judy and Aunt Connie give you for your birthday?" I asked Robby while Alphonse was in the backyard calling Bru and Der.

"Oh, no, Will! That was for Chip's new cage!"

Rob had almost forty dollars, and I had another nineteen. We went through the hall closet and checked Mom's and Dad's jacket pockets where we found four seventy-seven in bills and change. There was another forty-seven cents under the couch cushions and sixty cents at the bottom of the washing machine. We ended up with sixty-four dollars and eighty-four cents and all Mom's coupons.

I left a note for my mother telling her that if we weren't back by the time she got home with Dad, we would be soon. I also told her not to start dinner.

Alphonse was sitting behind the wheel of the truck when we got out to the driveway. Its engine was humming as if it had just come off the assembly line.

"When did you learn to drive?" I asked Alphonse after Robby and I got in and buckled up.

"While I was waiting for you," he replied as we roared out of the driveway backwards.

"Fifty–eight dollars? You spent fifty-eight dollars on . . . this?" Mom complained after we got home. She had just gotten through chewing us out for leaving the yard and getting in a sports utility vehicle with an alien and was now moving on to wasting money. Buying heavily processed foods filled with additives and highly refined sugar had to be next on her schedule.

"I can't believe what food costs on this planet," Alphonse told her. "I am shocked . . . shocked, I tell you."

"Where did you get the money?" Dad asked.

"It was ours," I explained.

"Most of it was mine," Robby objected.

"And we found some around the house," I admitted.

"You couldn't have found much," Dad said. "There hasn't been much money here lately."

"What were you thinking of . . . going out and buying all this stuff?" Mom demanded.

All of a sudden it didn't seem like such a good idea anymore. The beings who had overrun our home were much more intelligent than we were. They could manage interstellar flight. They had known life forms from all over the universe. One of them was a professor. And two kids were going to chase them off with one really bad meal? Or one really good one, depending on your point of view? What *had* we been thinking of?

"We're . . . we're . . . making the tour group a Thanksgiving dinner," I stammered.

"Thanksgiving isn't for another six days."

"It's coming early this year?" I suggested.

Mom picked up one of the packages we'd bought and shook it at me. "You're having hot dogs for Thanksgiving?"

"Well, you know how sometimes turkey gets so dry you can't eat it? I've never had a hot dog I couldn't eat," I explained.

"We can't throw away this much food," Dad objected when Mom said she couldn't serve what we'd chosen. "Let the kids serve it. They paid for it."

He wasn't quite so obliging when we asked him to cook the hot dogs on the gas grill.

"It's November," he said. "It's cold outside."

"They're the good kind of hot dogs," Rob told him. "The ones you buy for the Sons and Daughters of the Pioneers Encampment. There's no tofu or turkey in them, just beef and pork and lots of salt. And we got four pounds of them."

Dad told me to start heating up the grill while he got his coat.

"What are these little marshmallows for?" Mom asked.

"The candied sweet potatoes," I said.

"Where are the sweet potatoes?"

"Nobody likes those so we didn't buy any," Rob said.

Mom groaned and went off to put clean sheets on Miss H'ld'n's bed.

Rob and I had to wash and dry enough dishes for ten people to use for dinner. We got Alphonse to put the five frozen pizzas in the oven, and he arranged all the cheese puffs in bowls. That, with the hot dogs substituting for bacon, pretty much duplicated the meals that had made Corell Merqhors sick at the Sons and Daughters of the Pioneers Encampment. But just to be safe (and because we liked it), we poured four large cans of cooked spaghetti into a big pot and told Alphonse it was mashed potatoes and gravy.

"What if Corell Merqhors was sick with something else when he got here? What if he really had Tunella? What if he is the only alien in the universe who can't eat decent food?" Robby asked. I could tell from the tone of his voice he was worried about the forty dollars he'd contributed to our meal.

"That's why we bought these frozen breakfast sausages," I explained as I took them out of the microwave and threw them in with the spaghetti. "I ate a whole package once and barfed for an hour. And I love them."

"If this doesn't work, you're going to have to pay me back every cent I gave you with the money you get for Christmas," Rob warned me as he got ready to leave the kitchen with a plate of barbecue potato chips topped with spray cheese—a *much* better appetizer than the celery sticks stuffed with cream cheese that most people serve at the holidays.

I tried not to think about Rob's money as I sat down to eat. Instead, I told myself that if I didn't rid my home of the alien menace, I would at least get one meal I could truly be thankful for.

"This smells . . ." Klair said as she surveyed the table. "It just smells."

Dad and Rob took big sniffs and reached for the platters of hot dogs. I grabbed them first and passed them to Bru and Der.

"This is a traditional Earth food," I told them. "You should eat at least two each."

All the serving dishes made their way around the table. Everyone helped themselves but, except for Dad, Rob, and, I admit, me, everyone just picked at what was on their plates. I began to get nervous. The food wasn't going to do us any good sitting on the table.

Then I heard Alphonse sigh. He picked up a cheese puff, held his breath, and tossed it into his mouth.

"You really ought to try these," he said to Miss H'ld'n. "I've never had anything like them."

Miss H'ld'n looked doubtful.

Alphonse picked up a cheese puff and waved it back and forth in front of her lips.

"Here's the astro transporter approaching the space dock," he said as he got the puff closer and closer to her moustache, until she finally giggled and let him pop it into her mouth.

That got everyone nibbling at cheese puffs. Then Alphonse picked up a naked hot dog and bit the middle out of it so he was left holding an end in each hand.

"Tommy O. ate seven of those once," Rob told him.

"Is that good?" Bru asked.

"Very good. It's a big honor to be the person who eats the most hot dogs," I said.

"A charming custom," Professor Dorqus said as he used his fingers to bring one up to his mouth.

Alphonse had trouble figuring out how to get his spaghetti onto his fork, but once he managed to eat some, he said it went down smooth. I had a moment of panic when I saw how difficult it was for Bru and Der to get their spaghetti into their mouths. Those fat lips of theirs just slid off those slender sauce-covered strands. But Robby showed them how to slurp and the spaghetti disappeared in no time.

"And you all have to try some of this," Alphonse said after he'd finish a slice of pizza with a combination topping. "You'll know you've eaten something after you've eaten this."

It took a while, but eventually we finished everything. We washed it down with cheap colas, the kind that's often flat. I didn't want anyone burping and feeling better.

But I still wasn't done.

"Don't anybody get up!" I said. "We have dessert."

I ran out to the kitchen and came back with two Twinkie pies.

"We made them ourselves," Rob said. "Just now."

Then he went on to explain how much work it had been to open each individual Twinkie package and arrange it correctly in the pie plates. Everyone seemed impressed except for Mom.

"What's that on top?" she asked.

"The little marshmallows," I said. "We melted them. Doesn't it look good?"

"It certainly does," Alphonse agreed, though his voice had a tense, over-excited edge to it. He ate a forkful and sat for a while with his eyes closed. Then he took a deep breath, picked up the rest of his pie with both his hands, and shoved it into his face as fast as he could.

The other aliens followed his lead.

And that was it. The meal was over. There was nothing more I could do, I told myself as I watched my mother help Klair pat spaghetti sauce off from one of her earlobes. I heard my father try to explain to Professor Dorqus how canned spaghetti with frozen sausage became a traditional Thanksgiving food. I was aware that on one side of the table Miss H'ld'n had Alphonse by the hand and on the other Bru and Der were busily sneaking forks under the tablecloth.

It's not going to happen, I thought as I got to my feet and stumbled silently out of the room.

"Mom!" Rob wailed. "Will's trying to leave without helping to take the dishes out . . ."

The end of his complaint was drowned out by the sound of someone tossing cookies all over the dining room table.

"Tunella!" Alphonse shouted as he slowly stood up.

The cry made its way around the table as one alien after another lurched or crawled out of the dining room.

"Tunella?" my mother asked my father when they were the only ones left at the table.

Dad shrugged. "Can I have your pie?" he asked her.

The next morning the Thanksgiving group tour was gone, along with two sets of towels, six juice glasses, and all our matches.

My mother said Robby and I should be ashamed of ourselves for making guests spew, but anybody could tell she was just saying it because she thought she should. My father promised to pay us back for the money we'd spent on dinner the night before and said, since we'd saved him a repair bill on the sports utility vehicle, he thought he could afford to give us a little bonus. What with all that and moving back into our rooms, it was early in the afternoon before we got around to trying to make MTV come in again through the cable box. That's why we went down to the closet in the cellar to look for antenna wire.

And found Alphonse.

He was curled up in his blankets on the floor of the closet.

"I thought no one would ever come," he whispered.

"We hoped . . . we thought . . . you'd gone with the others," I explained.

"I'll be gone soon," he moaned. "The end is near."

"The end of what?" Rob asked.

"I'm dying. I hope so, anyway," he gasped.

"He does look pretty bad," Dad said to Mom.

"Maybe we should take him to a hospital and have his stomach pumped," she suggested.

"No, no. You . . . can't do . . . that. I have . . . two stomachs and . . . no insurance. Your . . . doctors are sure . . . to notice."

"Have you thrown up?" I asked. "That would probably make you feel better."

"Do I look in any shape to be throwing anything?"

"I mean has your lunch left your body the same way it went in?"

"I've never done that before. I don't . . . know how."

That was serious. We couldn't figure out what to do to help him.

"Hey! Let's call Aunt Connie!" Robby suggested all of a sudden. "She's a nurse and knows lots of disgusting things. I bet she knows how to make *anybody* throw up."

And she did.

8
One Alien is One Too Many

If it's true that all things happen for the best, then I guess it was a good thing that Bru and Der connected us to the Intergalacticnet while they were here. Yes, it meant Robby didn't get a very important birthday party invitation and neither one of us would ever be able to download shareware again. But it also made it possible for Sal's lawyer to send us that three page e-mail that included the phrase "terminating our business relationship." It was written proof that we were through with aliens.

Almost.

"This is just what we need around here—another guy who wears tube socks," Dad grumbled late one afternoon in January as he worked over a basket of clean clothes in the living room so he could listen to the CD player. "At least I haven't been seeing any extra underwear in the wash."

We looked at each other, the meaning of that statement settling into our minds at the same time.

Yuck.

Work had been slow that day, and Dad had come home a little early because he'd fallen behind on the laundry and there were no clean towels or socks left. I had to take care of the dishes in the dishwasher, and Rob had to dust the living room, or pretend to, at least. Still, we were all in a pretty good mood because we wouldn't be doing any of this much longer. Mom had only one month left of full-time work.

"You think Reggie will have dinner ready on time tonight?" Alphonse asked. He was sitting on the raised hearth in front of the fireplace eating an apple and watching us. "I hate to eat late."

We all did.

"Only a few more weeks and she'll be back to working part time again," Dad said. "Things will start getting back to normal around here."

We all looked over at Alphonse.

Well, maybe not actually *normal*.

Alphonse had left the closet in the cellar, but only to

go back to the sunroom off our dining room. He had totally taken it over, leaving his things (mainly *our* things to which he'd helped himself) spread over the furniture and hanging from the blinds. We weren't at all clear on what he did all day while we were at school and work, but we knew what he didn't do. He didn't put CDs away when he was through with them. He didn't close up the cracker boxes after he took something out of them. He didn't put things back in the refrigerator. He didn't turn off lights when he left a room. He didn't flush the toilet.

We had to do all that stuff for him.

"I thought Reggie could take me out to lunch once she's not working all the time," Alphonse said. "She could drive me over to that new laser tag place, too. I really have to get out of this house."

"You could always go home," Robby suggested as he tried to dust around Alphonse.

"Home is where your heart is," Alphonse replied vaguely.

We heard Mom's car coming into the driveway. Then we heard her running on the deck.

"Guess why I'm late?" she exclaimed as she came in the door.

"Meteor craters in the highway," Alphonse suggested as he spit some apple seeds into his hand.

"No. The principal called me to her office."

"Oh-oh," Rob said. "That's never good."

"It was for me. The teacher I'm substituting for? She's

not coming back to work! I can have her job for the rest of the year! And maybe next year, too!"

"They've got a lot of nerve expecting you to stay on like that. I hope you told them off in good shape," Alphonse exclaimed.

"I told them I'd be delighted to take the job," Mom said.

"Reggie! You didn't!" Dad howled.

"Of course, I did. Why shouldn't I?"

"You've got work to do here," I said.

"There's not that much anymore. Not with all of us pitching in and helping out. We don't need a person here all the time just to take care of the house."

"Dad," Robby whispered. "Do something."

"You . . . you wouldn't just be taking care of the house. You could . . . um . . . go back to giving guitar lessons and substitute teaching once or twice a week. You wouldn't *just* be taking care of the house," Dad stammered.

"But we need the money," Mom said.

"Oh, you don't have to worry about that. We got ahead on the bills these past couple of months, and Will and Rob got rid of the aliens."

"I did it, Dad," I reminded him. "It was my idea."

"What? What? What about my forty dollars? What about my help? Mom! Will is trying to take all the credit again and—"

Dad interrupted Rob. "The point I was trying to make was that we don't need Mom to work so much." He gave her a smile. "Why don't you just tell the folks at the school to find someone else?"

"Because I don't want to."

"But we want you to," I said.

"Yeah," Rob agreed, "we're tired of doing your work for you."

" 'My work?' " she repeated. " 'My work?' Why is doing *your* laundry, cleaning *your* rooms, picking up *your* things that *you* left all over the house and yard 'my work?' And what about shopping for *your* clothes? And taking *your* library books back to the library? And driving *you* to *your* friends' houses? When did all that become 'my work' that I have to do before I can do anything else? This is the Twenty-first Century, you know. Women have equal rights."

"Not really. If I remember my Earth history correctly, the Equal Rights Amendment to the American Constitution was never actually passed into law. The way I understand things, that means you are supposed to be doing our laundry, cleaning our rooms, picking up our things . . . all that," Alphonse told Mom.

That was the way I understood things, too.

"Ignore him, Reggie," Dad said as he made an awful face at Alphonse. "Of course you can take a job, if you want to—"

"I don't need your permission to do it," Mom broke in.

"I wasn't giving you permission . . ."

"Oh? So you don't want me to take the job?"

"Of course I want you to take the job," Dad said.

"No, you don't!" Rob, Alphonse, and I all shouted.

Mom stamped off to her room with Dad right behind her. Alphonse followed them down the hall. From the living room we could hear him calling, "When are you starting dinner?" and then a loud bang as someone slammed Mom's and Dad's bedroom door.

"This is bad," I said as I sank down onto the couch, still clutching the last dish I'd been drying. "Real bad."

"What if Dad can't talk her out of taking that job? What will become of us?" Rob asked. "We need her here to do things for us."

Alphonse agreed. "I am *so* sick of making my own lunch every day."

"Maybe there's some way she can take the job and do all the cleaning, too," I suggested.

"She sleeps too much," Alphonse complained. "And she doesn't need to practice playing the guitar so often. The average person can't tell if she's making a mistake anyway. What about reading the newspaper? She could stop doing that. There's nothing in there that anybody really needs to know."

"Yeah," Robby said. "There are a lot of things she could give up so she could do all the work around here."

"Helping you with your homework, for one," Alphonse pointed out. "Don't think I didn't notice how much time she spent helping you with that so-called science report. You were just hogging her and keeping her to yourself."

"She is his mother . . ." I started to object.

"And what about you?" Alphonse said. "It was your bright idea that she should take you sledding that day while you were on vacation from school."

"We got new sleds for Christmas! Weren't we supposed to use them?"

"You were gone almost two hours. Do you know how much work she could have done around here in two hours?" Alphonse asked. "You two have to stop thinking of just yourselves and let that woman get a few things done for the rest of us."

Dad came back to the living room. I could tell right away that the news was not good.

"Your mother has a lot of great ideas for things to do with the kids in her classes at that school, boys," he said as he sat down between me and his laundry basket.

"Does she have any great ideas for things to do with the kids in her house?" Robby grumbled. "Besides cleaning?"

"Why do you think someone else should have to clean up after you?" Dad asked. "What's so special about you?"

"Don't you think someone should have to clean up after you?" I asked him.

"I don't think someone should *have* to. I just think it would be real nice if someone *did*," Dad admitted.

"You know," Alphonse said, "on Yttrium 7 they put electrically charged rings in the ears . . ."

". . . of their slaves. Yes, we know," I said. "It won't

work here. None of us could ever hold Mom down long enough to get one on her."

"I'll help," Alphonse offered. "We could get her to do whatever we wanted with one of those things."

"Ah, but do we want her to do whatever we want?" Dad sighed as he folded a pile of wash clothes.

"Yes. Yes, we do," Robby and Alphonse said.

"If your mother does more interesting things, she'll be a more interesting person. And we'll all like that," Dad told us. He didn't sound very hopeful.

"No, we won't. Rob and I don't care whether or not she's interesting," I said.

Robby groaned and threw his dust cloth on the floor.

"Come on, Dad," he said. "Tell her she has to stay home. Can't you do anything with her?"

Dad looked at him and started to laugh. "I have never been able to do anything with your mother. It's what makes her so 'charming,' as the professor would have said. Of course, she has to take this job. Opportunities like this don't come along on most worlds."

"Well, all right," Alphonse said. "What about dinner tonight? She'll get that started on time, won't she?"

Whether or not she started it on time I can't say, but she wasn't *too* late getting it on the table.

Mom and Dad talked for a while about some things her students could do at their spring recital. Then there was a short pause during which they both looked a little nervous. Finally, Mom looked around the table at all of us and said, "I *do* understand that you don't like doing housework. I don't like doing housework. No one *likes* doing housework. I've been thinking that one thing that would help with this problem would be if we had less housework to do. And we'd have less housework to do if there were fewer of us in this house messing it up. One fewer to be exact."

"That's logical," Alphonse agreed. "How do we decide who will be the one to go? Draw straws? Fight a series of battles with the loser being thrown out of the house?"

Dad cleared his throat, then said, "We were thinking the one to leave should be you, Alphonse."

"That's sort of arbitrary, isn't it? Out of all the people here, why should I be the one to leave?"

"Because you're not a member of our family," Mom explained.

"Are you discriminating against me for not sharing your genes? I'm shocked."

"How can you be shocked?" I asked. "We've been telling you every day for the last two months that you've got to go."

"You were serious?"

"Yes!" we all exclaimed.

"It's not that we didn't enjoy having you here," Dad said. "For a while. For a very short while."

"But we're sick of doing your laundry and loading your dishes into the dishwasher. We have to do everything for you," Rob complained.

"I'm a guest. I thought you were supposed to do everything for me."

Mom laid her hand on one of Alphonse's. "That's right," she said gently. "You're a guest. And guests leave."

"Oh." Alphonse looked down at his plate for a moment. It was empty. He had cleaned it three times and had used his own spoon to scrape one of the serving dishes. Personally, I think that if there had been something edible left anywhere on the table he would have stayed a while longer. But there wasn't. So he silently got up, went out to the sunroom, and sat down on the floor in the corner.

"I can't believe he's going to leave," Dad said in a low voice.

"He hasn't gone yet," Rob pointed out.

I said, "I feel really bad about this."

"We just can't have him here forever, Will," Mom said.

"I don't want him here forever. But I don't want to feel badly about forcing him to leave, either. We're not just kicking him out of our house, we're kicking him off our planet. What kind of person does a thing like that?"

"A person who *really, really* wants him somewhere else," Rob said.

"Sometimes you have to feel bad in order to make something happen that has to happen. Do we want Alphonse with us the rest of our lives?" Dad asked.

We all agreed that was a pretty depressing thought.

"I want him to go, but I don't want to *make* him go. I want him to just leave by himself," I decided.

"Dream on," Robby laughed.

"If making him leave is something that has to happen, then we have to accept the bad way we feel when we force him to do it. We can make him leave, or we can feel good. We can't do both. Do you understand?" Dad asked.

I could almost feel the understanding coming, but I panicked and chased it off.

"What if we're making a terrible mistake?" I cried. "What if he's the last alien we'll ever know? What if we never meet another?"

"That would be alright with me," Rob replied.

"I don't think I can do this," I said as I buried my face in my hands.

Robby shrugged. "I can."

"Will, it's done. It's in the past now. You should be thinking about the future. And speaking of the future," Mom said, sounding like an actress pretending to be cheery, "I had an idea this afternoon after I was offered this job. If I work full time *and* keep giving guitar lessons *and* keep performing, we should end up with some extra money. We've never been on a long trip together. I thought maybe this summer we could go away for a few weeks. What do you say we drive to Orlando?"

"Orlando?" Robby and I shouted.

"The Magic Kingdom?" Robby cried

"Epcot?" I exclaimed.

"This planet's capital city?" Alphonse shrieked from where he was standing in the doorway to the sunroom. "Yes!"

Mom dropped her head onto her hand. "Alphonse, I thought we agreed you were going to leave?"

"I'm leaving to go to Orlando," Alphonse replied enthusiastically.

"No. *We're* going to Orlando. *You're* going back where you came from," Mom said.

"Not until after I've been to Orlando, I'm not." Alphonse hurried back to the table and sat down.

"You . . . are . . . not . . . going . . . with . . . us."

"You can't leave me home, Reggie. You need me. I'll help with the driving."

"You can get into a lot of trouble if you get caught driving without a license on this planet," Dad told him.

"I guarantee you, no one's going to catch me."

"Hey! Alphonse is right!" I said, relief rushing over me. "We do need him."

"For what?" Robby asked. "He never does anything."

"But he could."

My family looked doubtful.

"What do you mean?" Alphonse asked suspiciously.

I waved my hands over the table covered with our dirty dishes from dinner.

"I don't get it," Alphonse said.

"You could do our cleaning for us."

"Oh, no, no, no. I'm not a servant. I'm a . . . well, I'm not a servant, anyway."

"I agree with Alphonse. He should go home," Mom said.

"Think about it, everybody. Mom would have her job.

Dad, Rob, and I wouldn't have to do so much around the house. And Alphonse would stay. Everybody would get what they want," I said.

"What I *want* is to stay and do nothing," Alphonse objected.

"He could clean the bathroom mirrors and collect the trash. He could dust the living room. Hey! He could clean our rooms!" Rob realized.

"He could fix the cable box," Dad suggested. "I miss my MTV."

Alphonse and Mom looked at each other.

"I suppose I could do these things for you (some of them, anyway—you're never getting your local cable service back) and you could pay me. Then I'd have spending money for when we go to Orlando," Alphonse said, as if he were thinking out loud.

"You've been living off us for months," Mom yelled. "We shouldn't have to pay you a thing."

"We can afford to give him a *little* something," Dad admitted. "He can't go to Orlando without some money in his pocket."

Mom closed her eyes and groaned. "I am *not* sharing a motel room with him."

"You won't have to," I said. "He can sleep in the sports utility vehicle."

Alphonse, Robby, and I leaped to our feet, clapping our hands and raising our arms over our heads.

"We're going to Disney World!" we shouted.